THE VANISHING CHILDREN

Master Mercurius Mysteries
Book Five

Graham Brack

SAPERE
BOOKS

THE VANISHING CHILDREN

Published by Sapere Books.

20 Windermere Drive, Leeds, England, LS17 7UZ,
United Kingdom

saperebooks.com

ISBN: 978-1-80055-245-6

In Memoriam:
Dirk Smit
9 April 1931 — 10 November 2020
A man who loved Leiden and its history

PROLOGUE

With this slim volume of my memoirs, we come to my middle years, or what older men amusingly call their "prime".

Having passed my fortieth year, I was enjoying life at Leiden. As a result of my work for the Stadhouder and the King of England (who was rather more generous) I had a little money put by for the odd luxury, and the Stadhouder's favour meant that I was treated more gently by the university authorities than might otherwise have been the case. All in all, I was looking forward to another thirty years or so of pottering around the library and spending some of my evenings quietly in Jan Steen's bar on the Langebrug — not that much goes on quietly in Steen's place.

I have never been one to dance attendance on great men, but when they send for you it is very difficult to say no, largely because they don't give you a chance to answer anyway. William of Orange was a better man than many, but he had a carefree approach to the safety of others that I found disconcerting, especially when it was my safety at issue.

Anyway, if I do not set down my recollections now, nobody will ever know what really happened. I am aware that after each of these volumes is published there will be curmudgeons who dispute my account because there is nothing to support me in the history books. Well, of course there isn't, because until now their authors haven't had the opportunity to read my eyewitness accounts. But I shall expect better of them in future, always provided that the printers can read Van der Meer's handwriting.

Leiden, St Dominic's Day, 1721

CHAPTER ONE

I ought not to be surprised by anything that happens at the University of Leiden, but the summer of 1680 taxed my predictive powers to the full.

The Rector, Charles Drelincourt, having completed his term of office, showed absolutely no inclination to seek another. Admittedly most Rectors served only one year, but some of us hoped that such a literate, humane and enlightened man might have continued. Instead, the Professors chose to elect Friedrich Spanheim the Younger, presumably in the interest of balancing out these qualities.

As a matter of principle, I am wary of people called "the younger". They go through their entire lives being reminded that they have to live up to the reputation of "the elder" namesake and inevitably they fail, which leaves them with a sense of inferiority and bitterness that they then take out on those around them. At least, that was how it was for me with Spanheim.

Spanheim was a lantern-jawed man with a solid German skull and, I imagine, a solid German brain inside. Technically he was born in Geneva, but he was a German through and through. He cannot have been as much of a dunce as I suggest, because he earned an M.A. from Leiden at the age of only sixteen, continuing to infest the place for a while before going off to teach at Heidelberg. They tolerated him for fifteen years before he came back to Leiden as Professor of Theology and head of my faculty. I showed him the deference due to his position, but he was politely described as a man of "conservative views", and less politely described as a rabid fundamentalist devotee of

Calvinism. Spanheim saw nothing wrong with the idea that before we were born we were earmarked for either Heaven or Hell, and that nothing we could do would change God's decision. Admittedly that was orthodox Calvinist doctrine, but many of us struggled with reconciling this idea with God's love for mankind. Not so Spanheim, whose argument was that God is our father, and like every good father he gives his sons' rear ends a regular whipping for their own good.

The diligent reader of my journals will recall that in 1664 I had been received into the Roman Catholic Church secretly, and subsequently ordained a deacon at Troyes before being priested under the Bishop of Namur in Flanders, but ordered to keep it to myself so that if there were another wave of persecution of the Catholics he would have replacement priests to step forward. This may show how naïve I was, because subsequent cogitation convinced me that if Catholic priests were being burned at the stake, that was precisely the time when I didn't want to own up to being one; but, be that as it may, this chronology shows that I had some doubts about Calvinist doctrine before I came into contact with Spanheim. He simply converted those doubts into certainties.

To be allowed to keep my job I had to be an ordained Calvinist minister, which I was. It was just that, in true Ecumenical spirit, I had been ordained for both sides in this dispute. I managed to reconcile this with my conscience for quite some time, being visibly Protestant but secretly Catholic, but increasingly I ceased to act as a Calvinist minister. In theory we all had to take turns at preaching in the city's churches, but I started to forget to volunteer, and for a while nobody noticed. However, all good things come to an end, and when this clerical error was detected I came under pressure to return to the pulpit. It was becoming very difficult to preach doctrines about which I had grave reservations, but I was spared by the happy intervention of an elderly minister from Veur.

This little place lies a little over two hours' walk to the south west of Leiden, and had a very comely little church and a minister whose zeal was great but who was a hypochondriac. A couple of times he sent to the university asking if anyone could stand in for him due to some sickness or other, and I was deputed. It transpired that many of his congregation were themselves of a Catholic frame of mind, having been induced to convert by the peer pressure of their neighbours, and therefore they did not object if I never mentioned predestination in my sermons. Finding this a congenial posting, I reached an agreement with the minister to preach in his stead when necessary, perhaps three or four times a year, and on the strength of this arrangement I contrived to be excused from preaching in Leiden.

When Spanheim assumed the Rectorship, he saw it as his mission to stamp out any such backsliding and set out to promote a rigid Calvinism in the Faculty of Theology. Those happy few who have read the second volume of my memoirs may recall that I was sent by the Stadhouder, William III (whom God preserve) to Utrecht in 1674 to report on the recovery of his man Gijsbert Voet following a stroke or some such affliction. Voet and Spanheim had very similar views, so it was no surprise that Spanheim idolised the older man. Thus it was that he persuaded Voet's grandson, Johannes Voet, to come to Leiden as a Professor of Law in 1680.

I had met Johannes in Utrecht in 1674 and liked him. He was a moderate and highly learned man, and we had formed a friendship. Although Johannes was a devout member of the Reformed Church, he showed no desire to become ordained, preferring an administrative role and letting the ordained get on with it. He was a good friend, albeit about twelve leagues away in Utrecht, but I was not sure the friendship would survive his being under my feet if I ever preached to him.

However, one good thing came of this. When Spanheim heard Voet speaking warmly of me, he became convinced that I must be less of a liability to the faculty than he had supposed, and the pressure was momentarily relieved. How long that would last, who knew?

I have occasionally spoken disparagingly of the members of the Faculty of Law. It is true that they were devoted to spectacle and display. I have seen paintings of birds from the East Indies, one of which has a red cap and blue wings, with a green breast and yellow feet. Its plumage was comparatively subdued compared with some of my colleagues from the Faculty of Law. Johannes was cut from different cloth.

Yet he was so friendly and well-disposed towards all that in no time he had established himself as a valued member of the Faculty. His reputation — and that of his grandfather — had preceded him, so much so that Spanheim's endorsement did him no favours at all (though none were needed); and it cannot be denied that his public lectures were very well attended. He had a gift for expressing himself clearly, and many people who had no interest in law beyond keeping on the right side of it presented themselves at the door when he was speaking so that they could say that they had attended a lecture by the celebrated Professor Voet.

As befits a man of culture and learning, Voet lectured and wrote in Latin, thus ensuring that hardly any of my undergraduates had any hope of understanding him. Nevertheless, a select few were able to comprehend him, one of whom was so impressed he transferred to the Faculty of

Law and earned himself a doctorate. Johannes occasionally teased me by claiming to have stolen my star pupil, though in fact I doubt the young man in question had ever entertained thoughts of church ministry, being put to it by his father who had a parish somewhere. One thing is for sure; the student would earn more as a lawyer than he would ever earn as a minister.

I ought to add one additional piece of background. Since I had last met him, Johannes had acquired a wife. In May 1680, shortly before coming to Leiden, he married Magdalena de Sadalaer, of Amsterdam, a young woman of twenty-two. I have no idea how they met, but they were happy together, their comfort being assured by the fact that her father Abraham was allegedly a very rich man. I was not jealous. There was no man of my acquaintance as deserving of connubial bliss as Johannes.

Johannes had been at Leiden for barely a year when he was elected as the new Rector, the first of three terms that he was to serve, perhaps the only periods of my time at Leiden when I have been given the freedom of the Rector's office and my arrival there has not been greeted with an audible sigh.

As I said earlier, all good things come to an end, and after a year of gentle reform and improvement, he handed the office to Theodorus Rijcke, another young man and Professor of History and Rhetoric. Rijcke's term was largely marked by his impatience to get back to writing his major work, *Dissertatio de Primis Italiae Colonis et Aeneae adventu, Lucae Holstenii Notis et Castigationibus postumis in Stephani Byzantini Ethica, item Scymmichii Fragmentae antea non editis appendicis loco.*

The title gives away just how readable the mammoth tome was. Rijcke did not believe in using one word where six would do.

In his turn he was succeeded by Antonius Hulsius. Hulsius was another German, though none the worse for that. In addition to Dutch and German, he spoke Hebrew, Latin, Greek, French and even managed to master English, which many people from England do not appear to have done. Hulsius held the Chair of Hebrew, but his importance to this portion of my collected memoirs is that he was Rector when the events I shall describe took place; and it was to his office that I was obliged to apply for leave of absence without being able to explain truthfully why I wanted it, for reasons which I will now explain.

The alert reader will have realised that Hulsius must have been Rector in 1683-4 and, if particularly attentive, will recall that I was ordained in 1664, so the spring of 1684 saw the twentieth anniversary of my ordination, which seems to have been sufficient reason for the Bishop of Namur, Pierre Vandenperre, to decide to summon me to his palace; and since the messenger had been told to return with my reply, I had little choice but to agree on the spot.

I had never met this particular bishop, but he kept in touch with me via discreet messengers at intervals. This was one reason why any attempt to leave the priesthood would have been doomed to failure. Vandenperre would have found me wherever I went. Not, I hasten to add, that I had thoughts of leaving the Roman Catholic Church. While no Church exactly matches my theological beliefs, the Roman Church comes closest; but I sometimes wonder what was going through my head when I agreed to ordination. I had some romantic idea about having the care of souls, which has never actually happened, and on the few occasions that I have come across someone who really needed a priest I have been as much use as a glass mallet. This is especially true of women. I hate seeing women cry, and my natural response to their misery is to want to cry with them, which is not exactly the sort of spiritual comfort that they are seeking. More than one such encounter has ended up with them putting an arm round me and lending me their handkerchief.

I am not a skilled liar. If my untruth is met with silence I tend to blurt something out to fill the silence, and sometimes contradict my own lie, so it was with some trepidation that I ascended to the Rector's office. I had discounted the idea of claiming a need to visit a sick relative, because it was common knowledge that I had none, and telling the truth — that I was a secret Roman Catholic priest summoned by my bishop — seemed remarkably foolhardy. I would lose my position at the university and it was not beyond the realms of possibility that my next public appearance would be in front of the Gravensteen being chained to a stake while they piled faggots around me. No Roman Catholic priest had been burned recently but I was not entirely confident that the law had been repealed, and I had no desire to find out the hard way. Although I had a much-prized letter from the Stadhouder, William of Orange, describing me as his trusted servant and calling on all who read it to extend any assistance I might need to me, I worried that if he knew I was a Catholic he might even throw my letter in the flames himself.

Apart from anything else, Namur was one of the most awkward places to get to. Roughly fifty leagues from Leiden, I could walk it in around fifty hours, but there was no easy barge route and I was reluctant to hire a horse, since every horse I mount immediately slows to the point where I may as well walk in front of it. Even going by sea would not work, since there was nowhere in the lower provinces further from the sea.

However you looked at it, it would take me a week to get there and a week to walk back.

As a result of services rendered to the Stadhouder I had a little store of gold. [Manuscript note: Van der Meer sniggered at the word "little". I must not forget that.] I was reluctant to spend it, but hiring a carriage would be much kinder on my feet, and since I would not need to carry a week's food on my back, that looked like money well spent. I could walk to Rotterdam, take a barge to Antwerp or a coach to Breda, then make my way to Brussels where I might find a coach heading to Namur; or not, depending on my luck. But first I needed to explain to the Rector where I would be for three weeks of the teaching year.

The time-honoured explanation of a relative's funeral would hardly work, given that my grandmother had died four years before and even in our sleepy little village we bury people faster than that. I had no close living family and I could not claim to be disconcerted by the death of cousins whose names I barely knew. Inventing a family member for the sole purpose of claiming to be bereaved of them seemed morally questionable.

I paced back and forth in front of the academy building trying to think of a suitable explanation that would account for the urgency without provoking anyone into asking why I wanted to go to Flanders, when the hand of Providence took a turn, not for the first time in my life. I heard someone knocking on the window and, gazing upwards, saw the Rector gesturing to me to come up. At least I think that was what his hand gesture was, though if we had been in a tavern I might have drawn a different conclusion.

I mounted the stairs, still at a loss as to what I should say when I reached the top, only to find Hulsius standing in his doorway.

'You've saved me sending someone to find you,' he announced. Unusually he was in his shirt sleeves, his jacket hanging on a peg, presumably to avoid smearing it with ink since it was a sand-coloured affair. 'I have received a letter from the Stadhouder,' he announced, waving it at me as verification of his statement.

To say that my heart sank would be an understatement; it dropped to around knee-level. I could think of no circumstances in which the Stadhouder would write anything that concerned me unless he proposed to drag me away from my beloved library and place my life in mortal danger. Well, perhaps that was not his intention; but I had noticed that working for the Stadhouder was hazardous. I had done so twice before and escaped death in one case because someone intervened to protect me and once because the assailant had scruples about killing a man of the cloth, which did him great credit, though I suspect that as he dangled from the gallows a few days later it seemed to him to have been one of his poorer decisions.

'I do not pretend to know what is in this letter,' Hulsius continued, 'but my own covering note requests me to give you leave to wait upon the Stadhouder as a matter of extreme urgency and tells me that you may be gone some time.'

The word "requests" did not ring true. William of Orange did not "request" anything of anyone. Even if he said it, we knew what he really meant. Since he was Supreme Governor of the university, there was absolutely no chance that his "request" would not be granted.

'I need hardly say that this is most inconvenient,' Hulsius went on, 'but we must assume that the Stadhouder would surely not send for you if it were not a matter of the most vital national importance.'

Either that, or he had lost a set of keys, I thought.

'I am aware,' said Hulsius, 'that you have rendered some service to the State in the past, which redounds to the credit of this university. Go therefore with my blessing, Mercurius; and, whatever the task is, may your efforts be crowned with success. I would not wish a member of this university to fail.'

His eyebrows frowned so effectively they almost formed a V at the bridge of his nose. I was aware that I had not said a word, but I could think of none to say.

'Should I open the letter?' I stammered.

Hulsius was shocked. 'Not here, man! Your mission is of the utmost secrecy. I am told that I cannot be informed what it is, because it is so important and delicate a matter. Do not risk compromising either of us by opening it in my presence.'

I would like to think that this was evidence that Hulsius was demonstrating a meticulous scrupulosity about some State secret or other, but it is more likely that he just did not want to know anything that might prove to be inconvenient later. This way, if I failed and my dismembered body washed up in a canal somewhere, he could truthfully say he had no idea what I was doing in ... wherever I was being sent. I doubted that would be Namur, which was going to leave me with a major headache. In a contest to see which of the Stadhouder and my Bishop could be more understanding of my problems, both were likely to come second. Perhaps, if I were really lucky, it might be a short mission after which I could detour to Namur on the way back.

And pigs might fly.

CHAPTER TWO

I climbed to my chamber wearily, feeling all the cares of the world suddenly heaped across my shoulders, the only solace being that I had made my way there with a brief diversion to the dining hall where Mechtild was scrubbing the tables in preparation for dinner.

'Good day, Master,' she announced cheerfully, then, observing my countenance, she continued, 'Is something wrong?'

'I have to go away for a while. I was hoping you might find me a little something for the journey.'

'You must leave so quickly that you do not have time to eat with us?' she asked.

Mechtild's husband Albrecht was our kitchen master. If he had been at Sodom when the fires of Hell raged to its destruction, his first thought would probably have been that it was just the right temperature to make toast. Food that left Albrecht's kitchen was never knowingly undercooked.

For this reason, although we were all entitled to eat in the refectory for free, it was not unusual for a third of us to miss a meal now and again, even though we had to pay for the alternative. In fact, I suspect that the only reason some people ate there as often as they did was to avoid drawing attention to themselves as persistent defaulters. At least I had a legitimate excuse not to eat there for once.

'I'm afraid Albrecht has had to leave the cooking to me while he buys some spices,' Mechtild declared, which put an entirely different complexion on things. William of Orange could wait an hour, could he not? So long as he never knew about it.

'I'll just go to my room to pack,' I said, 'then I'll return to eat.'

Mechtild was not a woman of surpassing beauty, but her pastry certainly was. Those stubby fingers worked some kind of magic with flour and fat. Whereas I had once had a pie of Albrecht's making confiscated by the Stadhouder's guards in case I ran amok with it and killed someone with its crust, I would have to keep my bag firmly shut to ensure that Mechtild's pie did not fly off.

Once in my room, I carefully sliced open the seal on the letter to discover what doom lurked therein. The contents, while undoubtedly bespeaking urgency, were not very illuminating.

Mercurius,
As you love your country and your Stadhouder, please come at once.

There followed a scrawl which I had come to recognise as William's signature. Like that of most impatient men, it was always violent, jagged and compressed, but this particular specimen appeared more so than usual. The W, the two L's and the M were all spiky, and the other letters were not much better.

There was a postscript.

There is no time to be lost. Hire a horse. I will pay.

Goodness me, I thought, *things must be urgent.* Of course, saying he will pay and getting the money out of him might be very different things. There was a second postscript.

And not one of those animals you usually ride. Get one that can gallop.

This was an utter calumny. I am a cautious rider, that is all. I do not often have the opportunity to mount a horse and as a result of lack of practice I am, maybe, more circumspect than others when it comes to speed. Besides which, it is undignified for a churchman to ride at pace. Your hat is apt to fall off, even if you do not; and it was by no means certain that the horse would arrive at The Hague with me still aloft if I pushed him much above a trot.

I packed my bag, which took depressingly little time. I have few possessions apart from my books, and being a cleric I spend almost every day in clerical dress so I never have to think what to wear. I took a couple of books; if I were to be in The Hague for any length of time I could probably borrow books from William's personal library, where the volumes were in excellent condition as a result of never having been read. William was not one for extensive study.

I sealed my bag with a loop of rope through the handles, checked that it was not too heavy to carry, and left it near the door while I descended to my meal. There was an enticing smell, so unusual in those days where the university kitchen was concerned, with hardly any tinge of smoke. I was among the first, so I made to sit at a long table, only for Mechtild to call to me.

'Master Mercurius, your travelling meal is ready in the kitchen if you don't mind coming through.'

In another woman, her tone when making this statement might have portended some vulgar assignation, but when I followed I discovered the reason for her artifice. There was a place set at one of the kitchen tables.

'I hope you've no objection to eating here, Master,' she said, 'but I have a little something I keep for my special gentlemen, and I have no wish that others should see it.'

So saying she removed a cover to reveal a pie of the most lustrous golden colour, nestling on a bed of minted peas. Admittedly the peas had been dried and then reconstituted into a kind of edible sludge, but the smell was captivating. Mechtild poured me a cup of ale and left me to enjoy one of the best meals I had experienced in Leiden. It was fit for a Last Supper; and the thought came to me that if William's job was of the usual kind, it might well be my last.

After eating too well, I heaved myself off my bench and waddled to the stables to see about hiring a horse. Believing that mares are more docile than male horses, be they stallions or geldings, I asked if they had one available and was shown a bay mare.

I am no judge of horseflesh. Once I have counted the legs and satisfied myself that the animal can stand upright, my store of knowledge is empty. The stable master proceeded to remedy this deficiency with a lengthy monologue on the superior nature of all the animals in his keeping and this one in particular which, I was assured, could walk all day without fatigue, carry any load any distance and required almost no food or water to do so. He drew attention to various parts of her anatomy which were alleged to justify this encomium and named a quite astonishing daily rate for her hire. I offered him half what he wanted, and after some haggling we arrived at a number just this side of extortionate.

Her name, I was informed, was Fortuna, and any man would indeed be lucky to ride her. I duly clambered on and much to my surprise she did not drop dead where she stood, but showed every sign of being willing to carry me somewhere. In my amazement I almost forgot to ask for a receipt for my payment but fortunately recovered my wits just in time, and five minutes later Fortuna and I were following the Rijn out of town.

In good weather a man can walk to The Hague in about three and a half hours. A horse walks about half as fast again as a man, unless I hire the brute, in which event it slows to about three-quarters of my pace, but Fortuna showed no such inclination and once off the cobbles demonstrated a keenness to trot which was a new experience to me. Without any prompting from me she ambled along very happily, pausing once to take a drink and once to answer a call of nature — a delay not unconnected, perhaps, with the presence of a stallion in an adjoining field — but otherwise pressed on and, I judge, within a little over two hours we had arrived at the Binnenhof.

I showed the seal on my letter to the guards and was invited to come inside and give my horse to a stable lad while the captain of the guard was summoned to take me without delay to the Stadhouder.

Long before I reached him I knew he was not in a happy frame of mind. William was a small man and suffered grievously from asthma, as a result of which he had a weak chest, but he compensated for these handicaps by being vigorous and loud, not to mention wearing a breastplate as an ordinary item of indoor attire on occasion. However, to be fair to him I must allow that he was not capricious and rarely spoke roughly to those who did not deserve it. He was just aggressive to everyone.

The doors were flung open and I was announced, causing William to stop berating some poor clerk and advance towards me at pace. My inclination was to turn tail and run, but about five paces from me he came to a halt and lowered his bellowing one notch.

'Mercurius! Thank God you are come, and right timely too. I am threatened, Mercurius! I do not know whom to trust. So, of course, my thoughts turned to you, my beloved and loyal servant.' He lingered on the "loyal" as if to draw my attention to the fact that this was the most important word in that sentence, and then turned to the cringing clerk. 'Leave us! And send Bouwman in.'

The clerk hurried to obey, and soon we were joined by the Stadhouder's secretary, a man I knew, trusted and liked. Bouwman had succeeded to office when William had his predecessor hanged; admittedly the wretch had abused his office to plot against William and many a less enlightened statesman might have embellished the hanging with a few preliminaries such as public castration or boiling his hands in oil. To his credit, William had no taste for such frivolity and was entirely satisfied by stringing the man up with the minimum of fuss.

William invited me to sit, but I politely waited for him to do so, with the result that we both remained standing; or, more accurately, I stood while William paced and raged.

'Have you been to Amsterdam, Mercurius?'

'Not lately, Stadhouder.'

'A nest of vipers, Mercurius! Disloyal ingrates! A stew of pox-ridden sailors and clapped-up harpies! Lascivious, untrustworthy, grasping, conniving, money-grubbing Judases, the lot of them!'

I gathered from this introduction that they had done something to upset him.

'I am a patient man, Mercurius —' I may have flinched at this point in case God saw fit to unleash a thunderbolt of disgust at this perversion of the truth, but He let that one pass — 'who has given many years of service to my people when I could have been living a life of ease with no cares and perils, cultivating tulips with my beloved wife —'

I had never seen William so much as look at a tulip, though it was true that he had grown extremely fond of the Princess Mary, his English bride. I had been part of the embassy sent to England to negotiate the marriage and had been fortunate enough to spend some time with her, as a result of which there was no man who had a higher opinion of her merits than I had. These did not include spelling; even as a tyro at her language I had spotted several errors in her writing, and although she had taken steps to learn Dutch the average first former at Latin school would have tutted at her mistakes; but she had a good heart, an intelligent mind and loved William as much as any man was loved. William was equally smitten, to the point where he had hardly any mistresses at all worth talking about, and I rather suspected that those he had were kept just so that he did not let the United Provinces down in any international rulers' mistresses league.

'— but instead I am subjected to calumnies and the ingratitude of those from whom I should expect better.'

William paused to draw breath, leaving an awkward silence. I thought I ought to say something. 'I sympathise, Stadhouder.'

'Sympathy is not what I want from you, Mercurius! I want you to find out what these villains are plotting.'

I hated that word, especially when William said it. William saw plots all over the place, not entirely unreasonably given that there were plots sprouting all over the place. Admittedly his own agents fuelled some of them in an attempt to drag his critics into the open. There were plenty of people who thought that we did not need a Stadhouder and saw his election as anti-democratic. I had no idea what was going on in Amsterdam, neither did I want to find out, but it appeared that I had no choice.

'What do you know of Apeldoorn, Mercurius?'

I sensed a trick question, but I answered honestly anyway. 'The town, Excellency?'

'Of course, the town, Mercurius!'

'It is said to be a handsome town, though I have never seen it myself. It lies in the very heart of our country where the road going east from Amsterdam to Münster crosses the north-south road from Zwolle to Nijmegen.'

'Correct! A militarily strategic position,' William told me, though how he expected a minister of God to be impressed by that I have no idea. 'Not only that, Mercurius, there is a castle there, the Oude Loo. I'm going to buy it.'

Since William was always complaining that he was short of money I did not like to ask who would be paying for this, because it was abundantly clear that the population was about to be taxed again.

'I'm going to adopt it as my summer palace and let it be known that I intend to use it as a hunting lodge,' William continued.

'Indeed? I had no idea Your Excellency enjoyed hunting that much.'

'I don't, but it is a good cover for my real intention, which is to get close enough to keep a careful eye on Amsterdam, especially if I can camp a decent-sized army in the grounds.'

If the average man saw as many plots as William claimed to see we would call him deranged, but nobody was prepared to use that word to describe William. When you have an army people take you very seriously, however batty you may be.

'I blame myself for this, Mercurius. I have been too tolerant.'

This smacked of a dwarf claiming that he has been too tall, although I must allow that William was tolerant in religious matters. Actually, perhaps it would be truer to say that he was indifferent. He had no interest in favouring one religion over another, and it had to be admitted to his credit that he had been very welcoming to the Jews who had flooded into our country from Antwerp and similar places.

This requires a little explanation. The Spanish still owned the southern part of the Low Countries, including Antwerp, Brussels and Namur. Being keen to promote the Catholic religion there they had made life very uncomfortable for anyone who was not a Catholic, which included Huguenot weavers and Jewish diamond merchants, among others. Looking for a new home, they had headed north, in many cases to Amsterdam, which had now become the premier trading city of Europe. In barely a hundred years its population had grown five-fold or more, and there seemed to be endless land reclamation and building to accommodate these new arrivals and relieve them of the heavy money that they were obliged to carry around.

It is to the credit of my people that they dislike being made to conform in any way, and therefore they do not attempt to force others to do so, with the result that these newcomers still had their own separate communities in various townships. I assumed that William was about to crack down on the Jews, not an unreasonable assumption given that sooner or later everybody else did so.

'Have you ever heard of Rye House, Mercurius?'

This was beginning to look like an exercise in exposing my ignorance. I had never heard of the place. I could not even think of anyone or anywhere in the country called Rye. 'No, Excellency.'

'It's somewhere in England. I forget where, but no matter. The key thing is that it's near a racecourse.'

'A racecourse, Excellency?'

'Yes, Mercurius — a racecourse. A place where they hold races for horses. My Uncle Charles likes his racing, Mercurius, not to mention the other entertainments that he can enjoy away from the eyes of London.'

I began to get the drift. King Charles II of England was William's uncle, and a great one for the ladies. If every woman who had been bedded by Charles came to his palace at the same time he would need to build a substantial extension and, sad to say, quite a number would have travelled from my country. I was aware from my trip to England to organise William's wedding that many at Charles' court were great wagerers, so it should not surprise me that horse-racing was a popular entertainment.

'Some ne'er-do-wells plotted to ambush Charles and his brother James at this place Rye House, do foul murder on them and install the Duke of Monmouth as King. The difficulty is that a number of the chief plotters had been in exile over here, and Charles thinks that I had something to do with it.'

A not unnatural assumption, I would have said, but obviously one to which William took objection.

'I mean, credit me with some intelligence, Mercurius. If I'm going to encourage Englishmen here to murder their king, it would only be to put myself on the throne. I wouldn't hand it over to one of Charles' bastards. My wife has a much better claim.'

That could not be disputed, because William was married to James's daughter.

'The thing is, Mercurius, since the plot was discovered several more plotters have turned up here claiming to be Puritan refugees. I am loath to throw them out, because they could be very helpful if I ever needed to invade to defend Mary's right to the throne, but I need to know what they're saying. I don't mind them plotting against their own king, but I'm not having them trying to get rid of me. Have you kept up your English?'

As preparation for my trip to London some years before I had been instructed to learn some English, and I will admit that I continued to practise it when I could. 'I try, Excellency.'

'Good man! I want you to go to Amsterdam and mingle with them. They won't suspect you, seeing that you're a minister of religion. Find out what they're really up to. I don't have any animosity towards Uncle Charles, but if they're plotting against Uncle James I want to know about it. I don't trust him, Mercurius. He's an ardent Francophile, and if he takes King Louis' side life could get very uncomfortable for us.'

'Do you want them arrested, Stadhouder?'

'Of course not, you fool. If anyone is going to plot against James, let it be Englishmen. They would be welcome recruits to our side. Just don't let them get rid of Charles unless they get rid of James too.'

I was unclear how I was going to prevent another English civil war single-handedly, but those appeared to be my instructions.

Thinking that was the end of the interview, I bowed as if to leave.

'Where are you going, Mercurius? There's more.'

Surely not? Wasn't my life complicated enough?

'Our country is surrounded by rapacious neighbours,' William continued, 'and they are being succoured by vipers within my own bosom!'

This poetic image puzzled me more than a little, but since William was working himself up to a full-blooded rant I judged that I need ask no questions at this point.

'The French have to be subdued, Mercurius. They interfere with our shipping, they regularly declare war on us, and they encourage other countries like England to do the same. Deal firmly with King Louis, and a lot of our problems will fall away. And the only language Louis understands is written in steel. We need a powerful army, and I am committed to giving us one. Training and tactics have been improved, but I can do little more without money. And those parasites in Amsterdam are refusing to pay their taxes. They witter on about war being bad for trade, but I guarantee that if my army sets out for France several of them will rush to sell me peas and beans at inflated prices, not to mention arms and ammunition. The trouble is that they would just as happily sell it all to the French.'

'Surely that would be treason, Stadhouder?'

'Of course it would, and I would be within my rights to hang them for it. In fact, I've got a good mind to hang one or two now to discourage the others. They've invited me to go to Amsterdam to "discuss" the matter with the City Council.'

'That's good, Excellency. At least they're prepared to talk.'

'They can talk all they like, Mercurius. I'm not going. What kind of message does it send if a ruler can be summoned by a bunch of over-mighty barrow-boys? It would be inconsistent with my dignity to go.'

'I can see that, Stadhouder.'

'That's why I'm sending you.'

My tongue suddenly seemed three sizes too large for my mouth. 'Me, Stadhouder?' I finally stuttered.

'Yes, Mercurius.'

'But, Excellency, I'm not a diplomat.'

'Good. I don't want one of those bewigged fancy boys representing me. I want you to go up there and put the fear of God into them, and who better to do it than someone who knows God's ways intimately? Let it be known that eternal damnation is a certain fate for someone who plots against their ruler. It says so somewhere in the Bible, I'm sure.'

'The First Epistle of Peter, chapter two, verse thirteen,' I murmured mechanically. '"Submit yourselves for the Lord's sake to every human authority".'

'There you are, I knew you'd know it.'

'It doesn't say anything about damnation, though.'

William waved my concern away. 'It doesn't need to. We all know where sin leads, and if keeping taxes from your lord and master isn't a sin I don't know what is.'

My mouth was feeling very dry by this stage. 'Excellency, I am flattered by your trust in me, but I do not think I am equipped to bring this mission to a successful conclusion. I'm just a humble university lecturer, not even a professor. Why should they listen to me?'

'Because you'll be going as my personal emissary. No more trudging through the mud, Mercurius! We're going to put on a bit of a show. I'm lending you a carriage and a troop of horse. Bouwman will also give you a large jewelled collar to wear — I want it back afterwards, mind — and your expenses will be very generous. After all, you may find you need to bribe a few people.'

'But if the point of going is to get you money, why are you spending it on bribes, Excellency?'

William smiled and shook his head benevolently. 'You don't understand politics, do you, Mercurius? This is a sprat to catch a mackerel, a little investment to reap a great return. You can use the full range of diplomatic tricks — bribery, threats, imprisonment, sequestration of their assets, removal of privileges. Whatever it takes, Mercurius, you've got carte blanche from me. But I want those ungrateful money-grubbing leeches brought to heel! Public humiliation would be an added bonus, but the main thing is that they hand over the taxes in full and ideally with a fawning apology.'

I did not like the sound of this at all. What was to stop them imprisoning me, or worse? 'Wouldn't this task be more suited to someone else? Beniamino, for example.'

I did not know Beniamino's real name, but he was some kind of civil servant employed by William (or so he claimed) who persuaded men to give up their secrets by the application of branding irons, spikes and other inhuman devices. I had worked with him once and hoped I would never meet him again. Apart from being a cruel torturer, he was an abominable lute-player. In my nightmares I occasionally imagined myself strapped to a chair anticipating having my fingernails pulled out while Beniamino sang one of his disgusting sailors' songs to increase my suffering.

William winced. 'Unfortunately, Beniamino is not available at present. He already has a task on hand, and I'm not going to tell you what it is. That reminds me, Bouwman, we need to work out how to get him out of there before someone rearranges his bones.'

Bouwman duly made a note. Someday I should love to borrow his notebook to see the kind of thing William expected him to do. I imagined it would read something like:

Item, buy Princess Mary a new bonnet.
Item, write to King Charles protesting my innocence.
Item, rescue torturer from dungeon.
Item, declare war on France.

I thought I could see an objection to his plan. 'Excellency, if these men are as rich as I think they are, surely no amount of money we give them can make any difference to them?'

William smiled again. 'You don't understand finance either, do you? Of course it will make no real difference, but that isn't the point with these people. They exist to acquire money. Their whole waking life is devoted to its pursuit. I'll guarantee that if you walked through a market with a man worth a million guilders and he saw a chance to make five guilders more by buying some cheap fish, he'd do it. It's like a disease with them. They can't help themselves. A man could pity them for their weakness.'

Pity was not an attribute I often associated with William. Nobody showed him any in the years when the De Witts kept him from the Stadhoudership, and he was not about to expend any now that the De Witts had been laid in earth for a dozen years.

'Aren't successful businessmen clever?' I protested.

William considered this for a moment. 'Perhaps. But you're cleverer. They haven't got a doctorate from the University of Leiden, for a start.'

That stung. I had one, but William had ordered the university to give it to me. I had not earned it in the customary way. And, actually, he was wrong. One of the mayors in Amsterdam had a doctorate from Leiden, I was to discover; not only that, he had studied with Gijsbert Voet, Johannes's grandfather. However, none of this counted for much in the face of the

Stadhouder's misplaced conviction that I was their intellectual superior.

'I can't stand here chatting with you, Mercurius, pleasant as it is. Bouwman will take you to be briefed on the key people you will meet in Amsterdam and equip you for the journey. You'll also meet the Captain of the Horse who will accompany you.' He dropped his voice to something as close to a whisper as he could manage. 'Between us, don't rely on the hardware in the carts. Only one of them is full. The others have a thin layer of weaponry on top of a lot of bricks and rubble. Don't let anyone inspect them too closely, my good fellow.' He smacked me on the shoulder in what he probably thought was an affectionate and manly way but which seemed to me to be an exercise in brutality. 'I'll see you before you leave. Join us for supper tonight — my wife will be pleased to see you again. She often talks about you.'

Princess Mary had once suggested that I could be her chaplain when she came to this country, and I had discouraged the idea because I did not want to be where William could readily lay his hand on me. However, as the last few hours had shown, William could lay his hand on me anywhere in his lands, so I had given up a bit of a sinecure for nothing. Admittedly, my being a secret Catholic might have been mildly problematic if anyone had ever found that out, but I do not think William would have given that a moment's thought if I was useful to him in other ways. He could be my best protection were I to be discovered.

Bouwman coughed gently, a reminder that he was waiting to conduct me to my briefing, so I apologised for daydreaming and made to follow him.

CHAPTER THREE

When we reached Bouwman's small desk, he drew up a chair and invited me to sit before perching himself on his stool.

'It's good to see you again, Master,' he said.

'And I am always happy to see you, mijnheer Bouwman,' I replied, 'but I wish the Stadhouder would find some other favourite. This kind of mission does not suit me at all.'

'I fear that the position is a difficult one,' Bouwman opined. 'The merchants of Amsterdam are devoted to their profits of trade and will not see them diminished, as they fear will happen if His Excellency is able to prosecute his war.'

'But surely they see that if he cannot pay for his soldiers, their ships will be defenceless against the French pirates?'

'Certainly,' Bouwman answered. 'But, forgive me, they are not averse to arms and battle. Their ships are accompanied by gunships that they have hired. They simply object to paying the Stadhouder to do it when they can safeguard their ships themselves.'

'And what of their warehouses, their homes, their wives and daughters?'

'That is a very strong point,' Bouwman said. 'You may wish to make a note of it for use in your negotiations with them.'

I lowered my voice confidentially. 'What exactly has happened to Beniamino?' I asked.

Bouwman squirmed in his place. 'There are some things,' he said darkly, 'that it is better for a man not to know. But I do not think his captors will kill him so long as they believe that His Excellency will pay a ransom for him.'

'And will he?'

'The Stadhouder believes that making any such payment would merely invite further demands.'

'So Beniamino is lost?'

'Not exactly. The Stadhouder will not pay any ransom. But he may allow someone else to do so on his behalf.'

'Such as?'

'There is a gentleman from Burgundy who is skilled in these transactions. But I have said too much.'

'If this Burgundian is good at this sort of thing, why not send him to Amsterdam and leave me in peace?'

'It is idle to ask me, Master. I do not decide these affairs. And, I need hardly add, if you succeed you will be handsomely rewarded.'

'That's a moot point,' I grumbled, 'since I have as much chance of succeeding as a pig has of becoming Pope.'

'When one looks at the recent history of the Papacy,' Bouwman suggested, 'a pig might be a step upwards.'

This was a slur on the abilities of His Holiness Innocent XI, who was a particular hero of mine because he had condemned the practice of mental reservation — the doctrine which says that telling a lie may be permissible to avert a greater evil, as in when one tells a murderer that his intended victim is not at home; though, in my experience, murderers rarely seem to ask that.

If I allowed my outrage to show, it was dissipated when I noticed that Bouwman was smiling. The thought crossed my mind that perhaps he had divined my little secret, but he said no more about it.

'I am to tell you something of the people you will meet in Amsterdam, Master, but first I think we should seek out the Captain of Horse who is awaiting you. He has some matters to attend to before you set out and is anxious to proceed with them as soon as may be.'

I assented and meekly followed Bouwman down a flight of stairs I had never noticed before and across a courtyard to a large shed or barn. Inside a number of horses were being walked in procession in front of a large man in uniform who barked his approval of each in turn.

'May I present Master Mercurius, Captain?' Bouwman asked.

The military man turned and looked at me with the same sort of appraising glance he had just used on the beasts. I feared I was about to be sent to be reshod. His eye was all the keener because he had only one, the other being hidden behind an eye-patch of blue velvet.

He saluted me. 'Captain James Pringle, at your service.'

'I understand, Captain, that you and I are to travel together.'

'Aye, Master, to Amsterdam, where you will parley with those blackguards before allowing me to rip out their damned throats.'

I felt my own throat twitch at the prospect. 'I hope it won't come to that.'

'As do I. But we must be prepared, and they must be brought to believe that it might.' He looked adamantly determined. 'If it does, I know my duty,' he added.

He saluted me once more and turned back to his work. I did not know quite what to do, so I was grateful when Bouwman ushered me to the courtyard.

'Captain Pringle is very … military, is he not?' I offered.

'He is, perhaps, somewhat pugnacious,' agreed Bouwman. 'But we must remember that he is a Scot and make allowances.'

Bouwman poured me a beaker of wine. I am not a hardened drinker, but I needed something intoxicating after the day I had endured, and gulped it down, at which it was replaced.

'It may help you to know something of the government of Amsterdam,' he began.

I noticed he was not drinking. No doubt a man needed a clear head to deal with William, who was very abstemious himself. His Uncle Charles of England drank more while he was getting dressed in the morning than William drank all day; but then it took Charles a long time to get his clothes just right.

'Amsterdam is quite unusual in that it has four mayors. They are Coenraad van Beuningen, Johannes Hudde, Joan Huydecoper, Lord of Maarsseveen and Neerdijk and Cornelis Geelvinck.' As he pronounced their names he pointed to sketches of the men. Van Beuningen was a lean, cunning-looking man, with a sharp nose and a pointed chin. Hudde, by contrast, had a pleasingly open face, almost perfectly oval. Huydecoper had very dark eyes and hair and rather a superior look about him. Geelvinck had a receding hairline and grey hair showed beneath his cap. 'They are all prominent in the East India Company.'

I need hardly tell any reader about that sink of iniquity. The VOC, as it was known by its initials, was nominally a joint stock company in which its members owned shares, but it was richer and better armed than many nations and had a monopoly on trade with the Spice Islands that it was prepared to defend with arms if necessary. Given its enormous profits and state backing, it had no trouble attracting capital, which enabled it to grow and grow; and its joint stock nature meant that almost any sum of money could be invested, opening its riches to merchants who could never have mounted a trading expedition on their own. Meanwhile, the introduction of marine insurance meant that if ships were lost, the deficiency was made up by all those who participated in the venture. The fact that a family's wealth could not be wiped out in one afternoon tempted even more of them to invest.

Bouwman continued, 'Geelvinck is also a key investor in the West Indies Company.'

A foot in both camps! The GWC had been formed by men who, frustrated by the VOC's monopoly on trade with the Far East, had set out to voyage in the opposite direction, passing under the southern tip of the Americas and later to the islands of the Caribbean sea. The first GWC had been wound up, but a newer, better-managed one had been reconstituted in Amsterdam, and for a long time its ability to make great profits despite being much smaller than the VOC had puzzled men; then its horrible secret became known.

Some of its ships heading to South America had stopped to reprovision on the west coast of Africa. There they had been offered slaves taken in local wars. Realising that these unhappy people were not needed in the East Indies, but would be able to work in the crueller climates of Curaçao and such places, they had sold them there. For some time this was not widely known, but accounts of this trade had come to notice through the loose tongues of sailors and the discovery of shackles in the holds of returning ships.

There were those who defended this commerce, arguing that these men, women and children were already slaves when the Dutch arrived, but surely the discovery that my countrymen would pay for such captives can only have spurred more enslavement; and, in the way of such things, those enslaved were often the most peaceable of those peoples. I had read of clergymen who would argue that God intended that white men should have dominion over the black, and who quoted passages from the Bible to show that God had tolerated slavery in the Old Testament days. There were even those who contended that black men were not descended from Adam and therefore outside God's plan for us all, destined for Hell or annihilation of their souls as not being fully men. I realised, to my shame, that I had not given this matter enough thought. In my heart, I knew it to be pernicious and evil, but my feelings would not change anything. I must find some arguments to counter it. But it seemed to me that we consist of body and soul, and that when the body dies, the soul continues, to be clothed in due course with our resurrection body. The body is laid in the earth, and nobody had ever taught me that the soul had a colour, and since the soul is the immortal part of us all, I could not see how we could make a distinction that Our Heavenly Father had not made.

I realised that Bouwman was speaking. 'I'm sorry,' I said. 'I wasn't paying attention.'

'I was merely saying, Master, that perhaps I should give you these papers to read upon the journey, since we are coming close to supper-time and the Stadhouder and his lady will be waiting for you.'

I reluctantly agreed. I was in no mood for company, but perhaps Princess Mary would divert my thoughts for a while.

And a man has to eat, after all.

The Princess Mary would lift the spirits of any man. Not, perhaps, delicately built, nor pretty in the conventional sense of the word, but loyal and sensible. When William was away from The Hague, he was entirely happy to leave his wife to run the country; and his advisers knew only too well that Mary's word was William's word. Any attempt to drive a wedge between them would receive the sharp edge of William's tongue.

I was gratified to find that she remembered me, and that I was to sit at her right hand during supper. Apart from anything else, that meant that I was a long way from William, whose dinner conversations tended to run on martial lines and frequently featured discussions of the fate of King Louis of France if he fell into William's hands. Louis and I were born in the same year — did I ever mention that? — but then our paths diverged. He was King before he was five years old, and made policy like a five-year-old for the rest of his life. Even in the duplicitous, treacherous world of seventeenth-century European politics, Louis stood out as particularly slippery.

'I am pleased to see you once again, Master Mercurius,' Mary said. To my surprise, she spoke to me in Dutch. Since she had been in the country over six years I should not have been surprised, but we Dutch have become so accustomed to the English habit of expecting everyone to speak their barbaric language that it was a novelty to find an Englishwoman who had done otherwise.

'And I you, madam,' I replied. 'I hope that you have found our land to your liking.'

She smiled. 'Not at first,' she said.

When William brought her back after their marriage, ice blocked the rivers and forced them to land on the coast in a little village called Ter Heijde, a place so insignificant that there was nobody there who could lend William a carriage, so the party had to walk an hour or so to find suitable shelter.

'However,' she continued, 'I like it very well now. Has my husband told you that he is building a new palace for us?'

'He may have mentioned it in passing.'

'Unfortunately, we have not yet been blessed with living children, but it would be a good place to bring them up. So much healthier than The Hague.'

In my view, nowhere close to the Stadhouder could be considered healthy, but I let that go.

Our conversation moved along quite well, and I was pleased to note that Mary did not renew her suggestion that I might be her chaplain. I had a horrible feeling that despite my firm intention of refusing politely I might weaken and accept, especially if I thought I might have limited duties and plenty of time for reading and studying. I am not very good at saying no to women. Come to think of it, I am not very good at saying no to their husbands either, especially if they can put me in prison as hers could.

I was not well versed in court affairs, so I did not expect to recognise all those at table, but I could not help noticing that the Stadhouder paid a lot of attention to a young gentleman on his right. I was sure I had never seen him before, yet he looked extremely familiar.

The Princess followed my gaze. 'You have not been introduced to the Duke of Monmouth, I believe? He is the son of my uncle King Charles.'

Knowing that King Charles's heir was his brother, I deduced at once that this gentleman was an illegitimate son, but there was no doubting the family resemblance.

'He is newly arrived from England,' the Princess continued. She lowered her voice. 'I pray you, be very careful where he is concerned. Believe nothing that he tells you.'

I nodded to show, if not my comprehension of her advice, at least my reception of it.

'He is trying to raise support for his plan to seize the throne when his father dies, in order to prevent my father's succession. He believes that, as a Protestant nation, we will assist him to keep a Francophile Roman Catholic off the throne.'

'And will we?' I blurted out.

The Princess dabbed her mouth with her napkin. 'Dear me, Master, I am but a muddle-headed woman with no brain for politics. You must ask my husband.'

That was a patent untruth. Mary was not a silly girl, and I could not believe she did not know — and influence — her husband's mind.

'If, madam, your husband were to ask your advice, what would you say?'

I am sure I saw Mary smile gently as she saw through my little ruse.

'I think my husband might consider that helping people to depose their rightful ruler could set a dangerous precedent.' She slowly dissected an apple as, without looking at me, she murmured, 'And it will not have escaped his notice that if my father is displaced from the throne, so is his daughter. And so, therefore, ends her husband's thoughts of a throne.'

People have sometimes wondered how the English Queen Elizabeth was able to rule for over forty years without a husband's help. If they had met Mary, they might well have understood it.

She smiled once more as she spoke. 'It would be mightily undutiful in a nephew not to warn his uncle what mischief was in the making, would it not?'

'Indeed it would, madam.'

'To change the subject completely, I believe Captain Pringle is accompanying you to Amsterdam.'

'That is so.'

'That is good. It will give him the chance to see our land one more time before he and the other British soldiers return to their home country.'

For many years there had been soldiers from England and Scotland in our lands. They came and went as relations froze and thawed, but given that we had just a small army of our own, their presence had been comforting. The great thing about them was that their loyalty was never in question. They were unfailingly obedient to whoever paid them most. But it was always understood that if Britain needed them, they might be recalled at any time. If William was sending them, that was a clear hint to his uncle that they might be needed and, perhaps, the loyalty of his existing troops could not be taken for granted.

I was beginning to wish I had accepted the post of chaplain to the Princess. In five minutes she had taught me more of the state of affairs in my own country than I had ever understood before.

CHAPTER FOUR

Unbeknown to me a group of scouts had already set out whose job was to procure us lodgings on the journey. They planned that we should stay overnight at Lisse and then either arrive in Amsterdam at the end of the second day or, if necessary, find lodgings late in the day and arrive in a fresher condition the following morning. When supper was concluded I was taken to a closet where rich robes and jewellery were kept, but I declined almost all of them. I had no choice about the jewelled collar which was, it seemed, proof of my official status as William's emissary. I also accepted a dark blue cloak lined with the fur of martens, not because I am vain but because I expected that riding in a carriage would expose me to the cold. One of the drawbacks of living in a flat country is that there is little shelter from the wind.

I decided to have an early night in a comfortable bed and read my briefing notes on the journey, so I had just retired to my chamber when there came a knock at the door. Opening it, I found myself looking at a young man of about thirty years who dipped his head in greeting.

'Your pardon, Master,' he said. 'I did not realise you were abed.'

The cheeky rascal stood on tiptoe so he could see over my shoulder, presumably looking for a lady under the sheets.

'I wasn't yet. What do you want?' I asked, a little more sharply than I intended.

'I'm Kees, Master.' He seemed to think that this was sufficient explanation.

'I'm pleased to meet you, Kees. But why am I meeting you?'

'I'm your manservant, Master. I am to wait upon you as if you were the Stadhouder himself,' Kees announced, in a tone which indicated that he had learned that sentence verbatim from a tutor.

'Very good, Kees. I'll look forward to seeing you in the morning.'

'Yes, Master. Is there nothing you require now?'

'No, thank you.'

'A hot posset? More wood on the fire? Your boots polished?'

'No, thank you, Kees. You may go to bed.'

His face brightened at receiving a definite instruction. 'I shall, master. And I'll be up betimes to get you ready for the journey at daybreak.'

Daybreak? Nobody mentioned leaving at daybreak. I groaned as I padded back to bed. I like sleep. It's one of my favourite pastimes, but I have so little time to practise it.

Kees was true to his word. Even before the dawn chorus began, my door was pushed open and Kees entered bearing a pitcher of hot water and a plate of breakfast. There appeared to be sufficient food for a family.

'Have you had breakfast, Kees?'

'Of course, Master.'

'Then I'll take what I want and perhaps you can bundle the rest up in case you need something on the journey.'

He smiled like a child at St Nicholas-tide contemplating a new toy and a gingerbread treat. 'Thank you, Master!' He showed no sign of movement.

'You can go, Kees,' I said gently, remembering my sharpness of the night before.

'Don't you want me to shave you, Master?'

'I'm used to shaving myself, thank you.'

'If you're sure…' he said doubtfully.

'I am. Thank you.'

'Then I'll tell Captain Pringle you'll be there presently.'

I tidied myself up, dressed and packed my bag. I descended to the courtyard, hoping I would be able to spot Captain Pringle amidst all the bustle, but I had not anticipated what I saw as I opened the door.

There before me was a closed carriage drawn by two pairs of jet black horses. A liveried coachman sat above and two other fellows were clinging to the back. Beyond it a troop of about twenty horses were formed up with Captain Pringle leading the way. Spying me with his good eye, which involved turning a long way round in his saddle, he barked a command and the horsemen began pacing their horses on the spot. A second cart was standing a little way off which, it seemed, contained the luggage and impedimenta of our party, not to mention Kees, who clambered over the tailboard and made himself as comfortable as possible amidst the bags and crates.

I belatedly realised that nobody was going to move until I got into the carriage, which I hastened to do as quickly as was consistent with decorum and the tendency of the cloak to wrap around my legs. Once inside, I sat back and tried to make myself comfortable.

Due to the restricted view from a closed carriage I was completely unprepared for the appearance of four trumpeters who sounded a fanfare, seemingly about five paces from my ear, but then the procession began to move off, the troop of horse leading the way, followed by my carriage, the luggage cart and with four more horsemen bringing up the rear. I could see that they had their swords drawn. I could not imagine what mischief they thought they might deter in this way.

As we proceeded along the road I could not help but notice the deference shown to me by those whom we passed, many of whom removed their hats and bowed. They cannot possibly have known who I was, so I assume that this was an automatic response to seeing someone in a grand carriage who must, ipso facto, be a person of importance; except, of course, that I was not.

My discomfiture was enhanced a few hours later when I realised that instead of following the road along the river, Captain Pringle was detouring into Leiden. I slunk down in my seat in case I was recognised, and then discovered to my horror that the procession had come to a halt. The door to the carriage opened and one of the uniformed men was standing there with a little box which, apparently, I was expected to stand on in order to alight.

As I stepped from the carriage and tried to give the impression that I was not a complete novice at such a mode of travel, the Rector stepped forward, causing me to look up at the familiar portal of the Academy building.

'Welcome, Master,' he said, though his teeth were so tightly gritted I doubt if anyone else heard his words.

'Good day, Rector,' I replied.

Pringle appeared, having dismounted, and explained what was happening. 'We have to eat somewhere, so this seemed as good a place as any.'

'I hope you won't mind eating in a common refectory,' the Rector commented.

'I've been doing so for years,' I replied.

As we walked in, the Rector leaned over to speak softly to me. 'I've arranged for Mechtild to serve us at my table. It's better that way.'

I took it that he meant that Mechtild had cooked our food, in which event I concurred heartily. Anything which meant I avoided eating her husband's burnt offerings was to be applauded. When I went to London I saw some of the damage done by the Great Fire and unkindly felt the need to check that Albrecht had not been there in 1666. That our kitchen had not been engulfed in flames was a constant surprise to me.

As usual I waited politely for the Rector to take his seat, then discovered that he was waiting for me. The impasse was solved by Mechtild gently pushing the chair against the backs of my legs so that I dropped into it, whereupon the company took their places.

It was one of the most excruciating hours of my life. The Rector was uncomfortable about having me as his honoured guest, and I was equally uneasy about being so conspicuous when in company with my colleagues. I could see that Johannes Voet thought it all highly amusing, vexing me considerably by addressing me as "Your Excellency" and teasing me with enquiries about my plans to invade Sweden. I thought it safe to confirm that I was on my way to Amsterdam but decided all other aspects of my mission were confidential, partly because I had not yet read Bouwman's papers. A long carriage journey is highly soporific.

As the meal finished, the Rector could not wait to get me on my way.

'I don't think speeches are appropriate,' he snapped.

'I quite agree,' I replied thankfully, and we stood to leave.

The company stood respectfully, and as I walked past Master Hubertus, whose grasp on anything other than mathematics is loose at the best of times, I heard his remark to his neighbour.

'I never realised how much the Stadhouder looks like a fellow who used to work here.'

Willing myself to stay awake, I pored over the papers Bouwman had given me, and by the time we arrived at Lisse for our overnight stop I think I can claim to have mastered the details.

We put up at an inn, because arriving at a house with no notice might have embarrassed a host with insufficient food for thirty men and goodness knows how many horses, but an inn can be relied upon to provide something. I ate only sparingly; all that bouncing in the carriage had disordered my innards and I had little appetite, though I did enjoy a baked apple.

When I arrived in my chamber, I discovered that Kees intended to sleep at the foot of my bed. I was not entirely comfortable with this, but if that is what the servants of great men do, who was I to stop him? Suffice it to say that he slept rather better than I did. I could not accustom myself to hearing someone else breathing in the room and Kees seemed disinclined to stop, even when I petulantly ordered him to do so.

I had just drifted off when Kees woke me with some hot bread and a jug of water with which he proposed to shave me. For the first time in my life I allowed someone else to wield a razor near my throat, and I am bound to say that it was not an entirely unpleasant experience. Partway through it occurred to me that I had no guarantee that Kees was not one of the rebels who would gladly sabotage my mission, but if he had been about to slit my neck he had had ample opportunity to do so. Besides which, he was whistling as he went about his work, and I could not help thinking that a man who can whistle as he despatches another must be a rare specimen indeed.

We may have lacked four trumpeters, but it transpired that Pringle's company of horsemen included someone with a posthorn who deputised with a lusty little snippet of music as we took to the road.

The weather remained fine, if chilly, and we made good progress on the firm road so as to bring us to a village close to Amsterdam, where we stopped to have something to eat and rest the horses. An old man appeared from a cottage to remonstrate with us about the amount of grass the horses were eating, but when he saw the soldiers' steel he hesitated, and when he pocketed Pringle's piece of silver he decided that there was actually no issue to worry about.

I wondered how much more of this I must endure, so I sought some local knowledge. 'How far is it to Amsterdam?' I asked him.

The old man took one glance at the collar and cloak and instantly dropped to his knees. 'It's about three leagues, Your Excellencyship,' he told me, 'but in a fine carriage like that, you could do it in two.'

CHAPTER FIVE

The citizens of Amsterdam showed a healthy indifference to my arrival, as if to say that there was no reason for the people of so great a city to be impressed by a grand carriage and a troop of horse, and we progressed without incident to the Town Hall.

If you have ever seen the Town Hall of Amsterdam you may be prepared, as I was not, for its immensity. I have no idea what goes on there that could possibly justify so large a building. Walking from one end to the other would be a day's exercise for many men.

We came to a halt in front of the building. There was no welcoming party, and as the lackeys on the rear of the carriage dismounted to open my door Pringle ordered them to wait. Wheeling his horse round, he came back to the side of the carriage.

'I'll not countenance this disrespect,' he announced, and ordered the carriage driver to stand still while he formed up the troop of horse and ordered the riders to draw their swords. He then began to lead them up the steps as if to enter the Town Hall while mounted.

This produced the desired effect. The great doors flew open and a number of men tumbled out and formed themselves into a semblance of a straight line. One of their number advanced a few paces and waited by the door, at which Pringle nodded and the servants opened the door for me and waited for me to dismount.

'I am Johannes Hudde, Your Excellency,' the man introduced himself. 'Our apologies — we were planning to greet you within.'

If this was a fiction, as I suspect it was, it was delivered with such panache that it almost defied anyone to argue with it.

He quickly waved his colleagues forward, whom he introduced in turn. 'Coenraad van Beuningen, Dr Joan Huydecoper, Lord of Maarsseveen and Neerdijk and Cornelis Geelvinck, my fellow Mayors.'

Huydecoper took his doctorate at the University of Leiden, so we had something in common, except that I imagine that he had earned his.

Each bowed, Van Beuningen being the most enthusiastic, whereas Huydecoper barely inclined his head. I acknowledged them with a bow of my own, abruptly curtailed because I had forgotten the heavy gold collar which almost caused me to pitch forward as I leaned towards them.

Noticing a brooding presence to my side I made haste to introduce Pringle, who described himself as the Military Emissary of the Stadhouder. If such a position existed, this was the first that I had heard of it, but he did not appear to be in a mood to discuss such niceties, so I let it drop.

Hudde invited me to enter and take some refreshment in the great chamber, which was very fine. Pringle marched along beside me, accompanied by four men with their hands firmly on their swords. A couple of civic guards looked at Huydecoper as if to question whether they should insist on disarming their guests, but he shook his head briefly and we continued on our way.

In the council chamber I was invited to sit, after which the four mayors did the same. There was no chair for Pringle, but this did not discomfit him in the least, and he and his men helped themselves to seats and placed them along the wall, indicating that they were in the room but not in the conversation.

Hudde suggested that we begin with a prayer for the success of our discussions, and since I was the only ordained minister there, I took the lead. My prayer was fervent, because the sooner I succeeded the sooner I could go home, but I silently added a codicil to my prayer asking God to understand that my instructions left very little room for manoeuvre. To William's way of thinking, compromise meant accepting the other side's abject surrender gracefully.

The prayer being concluded, Huydecoper raced in like a wolf who had spied an unaccompanied piglet. 'This republic,' he announced, 'being founded upon democratic principles, looks upon the States-General as the sovereign power of our United Provinces, whose servant the Stadhouder is; and therefore matters of war and peace are to be decided by the States-General alone. The Stadhouder is not a monarch.'

It was quite remarkable that in around fifty words Huydecoper had managed to find at least five things that William would have disagreed with. The difficulty was in trying to articulate a response that would encapsulate his feeling; which, broadly stated, was that this bunch of rich boys could go and boil their heads.

However, I am not a moral philosopher for nothing, and one of the tricks of my trade is to harness the power of silence, especially when you have nothing useful to say, so I simply sat silently and waited for someone else to say something. As the silence lengthened, I could see Geelvinck looking increasingly uncomfortable and gesturing to Van Beuningen to say something.

'We recognise, of course, that the Stadhouder means well,' Van Beuningen began, 'but he must realise that prolonged and repeated wars are damaging to this country's interest, being, as we are, a trading nation.'

Feeling that I should say something, I cleared my throat and added a couple of words. 'Unjustified prolonged and repeated wars, perhaps.'

'Well, naturally, if the war were justified...' Van Beuningen stuttered.

'But this one is not,' Huydecoper announced firmly.

'How do you know that?' I enquired.

'What cause can there be?'

'It may be,' I suggested, 'that the Stadhouder knows some cause but cannot make it public.'

Hudde and Geelvinck looked concerned, as if this notion had not occurred to them.

'If there is some such cause, the Stadhouder has a duty to make it known,' stormed Huydecoper.

The image of Beniamino strapped to a rack while foreigners tormented him with hot irons came into my mind. It was imaginary, because I had no idea where he was or in what case he stood, but it was very powerful, and I could not suppose that it had entered my brain at that point except that I should use it to make my case.

'There may be a brave Dutchman who has risked his very life to obtain information touching upon the safety of the state which, if made known, would place him in great peril,' I said, seeking to do so in a tone of voice which said "Do not question me on this, for burning spills under my toenails would not cause me to reveal more." Needless to say, at the first sight of a burning spill I should have blurted out everything I knew on the matter, but they were not to know that.

Huydecoper frowned deeply. 'You mean that there is a Dutch spy at the French court?'

'If there were, you would not expect me to admit it, surely?' I answered.

'Come, Master, we are all loyal Dutchmen here. You can speak frankly.'

This was awkward. If I laboured under the persistent belief that I was not much of an investigator, it was abundantly clear to me that I was even less of a diplomat. How could I be? I have no skill in lying. Thus I fell back on my reliance on silence.

At length Hudde stood up. 'We are being unfair to the Master. He has, after all, only just arrived after a long journey and it is late in the day. He must be fatigued. I suggest that we adjourn to our own homes and reconvene in the morning. Master, I would be greatly honoured if you would consent to lodge in my humble home.'

Humble it was not, comprising as it did four storeys and a basement, situated on one of the great canals which penetrate the city. Pringle insisted on a military escort through the streets with Kees left to run behind with the bags, thus ensuring that it was at least ten minutes after I was in my chamber that a sweating servant arrived with my luggage.

I washed and returned to dine with my host, who introduced me to his wife Debora. They had not been blessed with children, but I was to discover later that they had only married in their mid-forties, Debora having been widowed twice before.

We dined quite simply, but very well, and separated from the others Hudde impressed me as a learned and prudent man, by no means a hothead. If I were to effect any kind of conciliation between William and these men, Hudde was the most likely agent, and therefore I set about winning his confidence.

He showed me a telescope that he had fashioned himself, and we were discussing the remarkable discoveries of mijnheer Van Leeuwenhoek when we were disturbed by a noise from outside. Hudde went to the window and looked out, whereupon I could clearly hear a mob chanting.

'Death to the Stadhouder! Death to the Stadhouder's stooge!'

Hudde was no coward. 'Be off with you!' he cried. 'This man is the city's guest. Be about your business!' He closed the window. 'The devil!' he said. 'How did they know you were here?'

Perhaps the twenty armed men accompanying the ornate carriage gave it away, I thought, but I said nothing. I was puzzled about a different matter. The people had been indifferent to me as I passed through the city earlier. Why had they suddenly become animated about my presence?

I cannot say that I slept well, despite the comfort of the chamber and, particularly, the feather bed. My mind refused to stop turning over the information I had been given and raising new questions. I was as sure as I could be that the mob of the night before had been bribed; I could see no other way to account for the sudden change of mood towards me; but in whose interest was it to whip up such sentiments? Was I supposed to be frightened by such a display?

Now, let it be said that I am no hero. I am not the man to face down a howling mob, and I have long felt that people are unduly severe on Pontius Pilate in that regard. It ill becomes men to criticise him for bowing to pressure to crucify Jesus when those same men submit meekly under challenge in their own lives. However, while I might have been cowed in normal circumstances, the knowledge that Pringle and his men were on hand to protect me afforded me much comfort. This was enhanced by conversations we had shared on the journey, during which Pringle had regaled me with tales from his military past, many of which seemed to me to evidence an unhealthy delight in running people through with his sword. Faced with an adversary threatening me, Pringle would not think twice about despatching him; and some of his soldiers appeared incapable of thinking once.

When morning came, I took some time over my shaving and dressing to ensure that I cut as commanding a figure as I could. I should have liked to have been a hand or so taller, though William himself stood only five and a half feet and was touchy about references to his height (or lack of it). He would probably have told me I was tall enough.

I came down to breakfast where I was greeted very civilly by my host and his lady, who had politely waited until I appeared before eating anything. They asked me to say Grace, which I did, and we began to eat.

There is probably no clearer evidence of the divide in the world betwixt poor and rich than in the bread they eat. I grew up eating dark bread made from a mixture of flour according to what we could get; in the university we ate good white bread, but it was not as fine as that now set before me. My late grandmother, who ended her life in a sadly deficient dental state, could easily have managed to chew this fluffy comestible.

During my brief stay in France, I observed that some of the higher class of ladies there esteem it important to eat as little as possible so that they present a lean, willowy frame upon which their female attributes appear more impressive. By contrast, most Dutch women believe that good food is there to be eaten. Debora was definitely of this opinion. Long after I had eaten my fill, she was still delicately chewing anything put in front of her.

'Is the food not to your taste, Master?' she asked.

'No, it's excellent, I assure you,' I responded. 'Forgive me, at the university we are not accustomed to being so well provided for.'

'The university? Which is that, pray?'

'Leiden.'

'I did not realise that you were a university man,' she continued, leaving it unclear whether she thought that was a good or bad thing. It occurred to me that her husband had probably not been told that either, and perhaps I should not have said anything and left some mystery about my antecedents.

We were interrupted by the appearance of one of the maids, who addressed her master.

'Mijnheer, there is a man at the door asking to speak to the Master.'

Hudde frowned. 'A man? Do we know him?'

'No, mijnheer.' The maid dropped her voice. Undoubtedly she would have whispered, had it been feasible to make herself heard while maintaining a respectful distance. 'He is a Portuguese.'

Hudde rose from his chair. 'By your leave, Master, I will see who this man is and what he wants of you. I am sorry that your peace has been disturbed in this way.'

He departed the room and I could hear discussion in the hallway before he returned accompanied by a young man, who bowed deeply. He was dressed as we were, the distinguishing feature being a small black skullcap fixed to his hair with a silver clip. It was then I realised what the maid had meant.

The majority of Jews in Amsterdam are refugees from Spain and Portugal, and many of them are prosperous, having arrived here with their savings and having professions or trades that have enabled them to earn their living. There are some poorer Jews from the Baltic coast and Germany who do not mix much with them, I understand, and who seem to speak a different language.

Since my country and Spain have often been at war, those Jews who come from there prefer to describe themselves as Portuguese — and insofar as their port of embarkation is often Lisbon, they are not untruthful.

'I am Israel Pereyra,' the young man began.

'Pereyra? You are a kinsman of Abraham Pereyra?' Hudde interrupted.

I discovered later that Abraham Pereyra was reputed one of the richest and most pious men in Amsterdam. There were plenty of rich men there, but not so many pious ones.

'Not in the blood line, mijnheer. He is a cousin of my father.'

'You wished to speak to me, mijnheer Pereyra,' I said.

'I beg you will forgive the interruption. I will wait upon you some other time if it is inconvenient, but I could not miss the opportunity to speak to the representative of our beloved Stadhouder.'

If this seems a surprising mode of speech, it should be noted that these Jews are peculiarly attached to the Stadhouder, holding him responsible for granting them protection and liberty in our country. Admittedly it was a different Stadhouder who let them come in the first place, but they seem to transfer the gratitude to each successive incumbent.

'I will be pleased to hear you,' I answered.

'I think perhaps we should withdraw,' Hudde suggested, motioning to his wife.

'There is no need on my account,' Pereyra replied. 'It would be impolite to cause you to quit a room in your own house, and what I have to say may be heard by anyone. Master, we are loyal subjects of the Stadhouder but we are not receiving justice here. Knowing him to be a fair and honest lord, we are sure that if he knew of our cause he would grant us his full attention and care; therefore, I wish to lay before you our complaint, trusting that you will make it known to him.'

I may have gulped at this point. At least, I tried to disguise the fact that I was gulping and broke into a coughing fit. 'Of course,' I finally wheezed, and immediately wished that I had not.

'You will speak to the Stadhouder for us?'

'I meant of course I'll listen to you and then see what the best course of action is.' I could see Pereyra's expression indicating that he thought he was being fobbed off, so I moved to restore his confidence. 'I have wide powers from the Stadhouder, and it may be that I can manage the matter myself.'

There is an expression "to put your foot in your mouth", I believe. This was an exercise in putting both feet in, halfway up the legs. Why do I say these things?

Pereyra came straight to the point. 'Three Jewish children have disappeared. We believe that they have been abducted and may still be living. But the authorities insist that all three must have suffered accidents. We cannot get the matter properly investigated.'

I looked at Hudde, who adopted a pained expression.

'I assure you, mijnheer, if there were a shred of evidence…'

'There is no evidence because nobody has looked for it!' Pereyra exclaimed.

I hate argument; well, not scholarly argument, obviously, because that's what I spend my days doing, but workaday unprofessional argument. Conflict is uncomfortable to me, so I decided to try to defuse this spat before it grew any larger.

'Mijnheer Pereyra, mijnheer Hudde and I must be about the Stadhouder's business now, but if you will tell me where to find you I will listen to you at greater length when I can, and I promise that you and your people will be able to lay any matter you wish before me before I leave Amsterdam.'

'And you will put it before the Stadhouder?'

'I am the Stadhouder's chosen investigator,' I announced. 'I will look into the matter myself.'

If my feet were in my mouth before, I was now close to swallowing my own backside. But I would have the reader know that it was not vanity that made me speak so; it was the certain knowledge that if I laid it before William he would send me back to investigate it anyway.

I was just saving myself a long carriage ride.

CHAPTER SIX

The four mayors were very animated. They took it in turns to try to browbeat me into seeing things their way then, when that failed, they tried speaking at the same time. I remained resolutely silent, reasoning that so long as I said nothing, I would not reveal that I also knew nothing.

This is where the Reformed Protestants are at a disadvantage. Since they eschew bishops, they do not know what truly inflexible behaviour looks like. As I have remarked earlier, I had little contact with my own bishop, nor with the bishops of the Dutch Mission based in Utrecht (who probably did not know of my existence) but I had met a couple while I was studying and their ability to conclude an argument by simply saying "I have said what I have said" was quite breathtaking. It occurred to me that this was the sort of approach that William would expect his emissary to take, so I was just biding my time until I had to say something.

Huydecoper was exasperated. 'This is not a negotiation!' he stormed. 'All the points are being made by one side.'

'You are quite right,' I replied, as calmly as I could. 'My master's view is that there is nothing to negotiate.'

'Then he won't get his taxes!' Geelvinck announced.

'Do you deny,' I asked, 'that the Stadhouder is charged with managing the external affairs of these states?'

'Of course not,' Geelvinck began.

I interrupted at once. I find it very irritating when people do that to me, so I assumed they would be equally annoyed when I did it. 'And is, or is not, the Kingdom of France abroad?'

'Of course it is,' Geelvinck spluttered, 'but…'

'Then matters of war and peace with France are self-evidently within the purview of the Stadhouder.'

'Yes, but not the mode of paying for them,' Huydecoper protested.

'The one must encompass the other,' I remarked mildly. 'There would be no point in giving the Stadhouder the powers you have just agreed that he has if he has no practical way of using them.'

'The Stadhouder has been badly advised,' Van Beuningen suggested. 'We do not doubt his good intentions, but he is set upon a course injurious to the best interests of this nation.'

'You mean of the East India Company,' I commented.

'Not at all! Well, yes, but that is not the point. All trade is hampered by war in the North Sea, and we are a trading nation. Businesses will wither in the event of a prolonged war.'

'Exactly,' I answered. 'So if you want a short war, you would be well advised to see the Stadhouder provided with overwhelming forces so that he can gain a quick victory.'

'We don't want any kind of war,' argued Huydecoper. 'I am surprised that a man of God should be promoting the idea of violence as a means of resolving differences between nations.'

'I am not,' I said. 'I hope that we will provide so powerful a force that our enemy will realise the futility of resistance and capitulate without a drop of blood being shed.' I was feeling quite smug at this point. *Diplomacy is not as difficult as I feared*, I thought.

Hudde decided that he ought to try acting as peacemaker. 'Master Mercurius, you must not suppose that we wish to oppose the Stadhouder for any other reason than to do our duty as guardians of the best interests of our city.'

'It just happens that those appear to coincide with those of our enemy,' I remarked.

'We are elected to secure the prosperity of the city, and that means that we must trade peaceably,' Hudde continued.

'And if the French invade again, how much trade do you think Amsterdam will be doing?' I asked. 'And who will receive the profit?'

'But there is no evidence that France is intending to invade,' Huydecoper snapped.

'It is only six years since we signed a peace treaty with France to conclude six years of war,' I remarked, 'and what has happened since that treaty was signed? France has annexed Strasbourg and Luxembourg. Do you not think this places our country in peril?'

'The French assure us that they are only retrieving land omitted from specific mention in the Treaty of Nijmegen to secure their own borders against attack,' Huydecoper answered.

'Attack? From whom? It cannot be the Spanish, because they would not pass through either city if attacking from the Spanish Netherlands. It cannot be France's German allies. And so far as I am aware, the Bishop of Liège has never expressed any animosity towards France.'

Even by the standards of the hierarchy of the Roman Catholic Church, Maximilian Henry, Bishop of Liège, was a shifty piece of work. Simultaneously Archbishop-Elector of Cologne, Bishop of Hildesheim and Bishop of Münster as well as Bishop of Liège, he was largely responsible for putting together the coalition of nations that attacked our country in the late war. It was widely rumoured that he was receiving substantial bribes from France. If he had any plans to treacherously attack that country, it could only be because he feared losing his touch if he did not practise his deceptions regularly. I might have been a Roman Catholic myself, but I could not excuse the double dealing of the quadruple bishop. I sometimes wondered if he had stopped reading when he got to the end of the ninth commandment, because his ability to covet his neighbour's ox and all his other possessions was unparalleled.

Huydecoper did not reply. He knew I had a point. The French were clearly preparing for another war by securing their eastern frontier.

'I think,' Hudde intervened, 'that matters are getting a little heated and perhaps we should take a little while for reflection before continuing.' There was general agreement to this proposal. 'Shall we resume later this afternoon?' he asked.

We agreed to reconvene at five o'clock. This was good because it gave me time to make good on my promise to visit mijnheer Pereyra to see what he was talking about, so I politely declined Hudde's invitation to dine with him, explaining what I proposed to do, and walked out of the building with Pringle following close behind.

'If you want any of them taught a salutary lesson, just let me know,' Pringle said. 'Such disrespect to the Stadhouder! If I string one of them up from a ship's yardarm it'll soon bring the rest in line.'

'Thank you, Captain,' I responded, 'but I'd rather convince them than kill them.'

Pringle shrugged. 'As you wish. But killing one is sure to convince the other three.'

Yours is a very straightforward world, isn't it? I thought.

Israel Pereyra was in his warehouse as he had promised. It was unusually constructed because it had a second tier of shelving on which barrels and large jars stood. They could be walked to the end where a gentle ramp brought them down to street level, which allowed his warehouse to hold much more than one might have thought from the outside. I could see casks of wine from Spain and Portugal, and olive oil, not to mention expensive fragrances from the countries bordering the Middle Sea. The room smelled wonderful.

Pereyra had removed his coat and had his sleeves rolled up as he dipped his hand into a small barrel. 'Excuse me one moment, Master,' he said. 'I'm just checking this saffron is good all the way down. Sometimes the villains put poor quality stuff at the bottom.' He drew up a handful, sniffed it and held it up to the light. 'That'll do,' he said, and returned it to the barrel for his clerk to reseal.

He resumed his coat and invited me to sit. 'May I offer you some refreshment? You will not be offended if I do not join you.'

I knew that Jews had some prohibions on eating and drinking, so I had not expected to be offered anything. 'Thank you, but let us get straight to the point, mijnheer Pereyra.'

'Very good. Then I will tell you plainly that three children have disappeared in recent months. All were in good health, all very young, and yet the city authorities refuse to investigate. They claim that the children must have wandered off and fallen in a canal.'

You are never far from a canal in Amsterdam, so there was some plausibility in this.

'But everyone who falls in a canal appears again sooner or later, and they have not floated the surface,' Pereyra continued. 'And our children are taught from a very early age not to leave our side. Even in a tolerant country such as this, we keep to our own neighbourhoods and our children do not stray far from home unaccompanied.'

I could see the truth in this. While I have very little experience of Jews, most foreigners seem to confine themselves to their own enclaves. The English in Leiden were an exception in that regard.

'Who were these children, and when did they disappear?' I asked.

Pereyra produced a small sheet of paper from a drawer of his desk. 'I have the details here,' he remarked.

The handwriting was beautiful. Many a clerk would have envied so clear and flowing a hand. I had to remind myself that it was the content and not the appearance that mattered.

Isidore de Espinosa, aged 2 years and 2 months, the son of Baruch and Rebecca. Taken from a courtyard behind their house, the second day of November, 1683.

Shmuel Pimentel, aged 2 years and 8 months, the son of Saul and Rachel. Last seen on the doorstep of their house, the eighteenth day of February, 1684.

Daniel Morteira, aged 11 months, the son of Abraham and Esther. Taken from his crib, the seventh day of April, 1684.

'All boys, I see,' I said.
'All boys,' Pereyra confirmed.
'Were there any witnesses?'
'Not that would help us much in finding the culprits. But I am not an investigator. Perhaps Your Excellency would like to speak to the parents yourself?'

I felt doubly uneasy; first, because I disliked the honorific title, and second, because I sensed expectations being raised that I was unlikely to meet. On the other hand, if I drew it to William's attention I knew exactly what would happen next. 'That would be good,' I replied. 'Do they all speak Dutch?'

'To some degree, but if you wish I will come to interpret for you.'

'Thank you. And please don't call me Your Excellency. I'm just Master Mercurius, of the University of Leiden.'

'As you wish. But I'm sure that if our beloved Stadhouder reposes his confidence in you, the word "just" is misplaced.' Pereyra smiled. He seemed genuinely friendly towards me, which made him a member of a very small clique in Amsterdam.

I left the warehouse with Pereyra, but we had gone only a few steps when Pringle hailed me.

'You're surely not intending to walk?' he asked.

'Of course. I walk everywhere. I don't usually have the luxury of a carriage. And I have spent too long sitting down recently. I need to stretch my legs.'

'That's as may be,' Pringle argued, 'but if you travel on foot in Amsterdam, these people will think you are of no account. The dignity of your office requires a carriage and escort.'

'But what of mijnheer Pereyra?'

Pringle sighed. 'I suppose he can ride in the carriage too, if he keeps out of sight.'

The door was opened for us, we climbed in, settled ourselves in our seats, and the carriage began to move.

'Stop!' said Pereyra.

'Stop? Why?'

'This is the place,' he said.

We had gone no more than ten paces.

'So close?'

'I wasn't given the chance to tell you,' he said with a twinkle in his eyes. 'The Espinosa family live in the street behind the warehouse.'

We solemnly alighted and Pereyra indicated a small archway between the buildings. I walked forward, plucking up my robe because you never know what noisome substances may lie beneath your feet. In fact, the street was very clean and tidy, as I remarked to Pereyra.

'The Law of Moses tells us that we must not leave filth where God may walk, and that he abhors any uncleanness.'

'The Law of Moses forms part of our holy book too, but a lot of Christians seem not to have read that part,' I replied.

Pereyra stopped at the door of a substantial house and knocked. Before entering he pressed his hand against a little box on the doorpost and said a few words of Hebrew. My Hebrew is extremely rusty, not to mention being biblical Hebrew rather than colloquial Hebrew, but I gathered that he was blessing someone or something.

'This is Master Mercurius,' Pereyra explained. 'He is a righteous man who is going to help us find out what has happened to Isidore.'

I did not remember having committed myself quite that far, but it was very clear that the grieving parents were overcome by the thought of help from any quarter. Baruch de Espinosa began to wail most alarmingly while his wife beat her breast with a clenched fist. After a little while Pereyra invited them to compose themselves and tell their story.

They began by confirming the date of Isidore's disappearance.

'I don't suppose you have a portrait of him?' I asked.

'His image is written on my heart,' replied Rebecca, and began sobbing again.

'Let me ask that another way,' I tried. 'How will we recognise him if we find him? Does he know his name?'

Baruch understood my question. 'He comes to us when we call Isidore.'

'I know that this is painful to you, but can you tell me what happened as precisely as you can?'

Baruch gathered himself and began his account. 'It was around the eighth hour.'

'Two in the afternoon?'

'Perhaps a little later. Isidore had eaten with us. In the morning he sits with Rebecca to learn from her. She teaches him to count, the shapes of letters, and so on. But that is enough for one so young, so after the midday meal he is allowed to play in the courtyard at the back of the house.'

'May I see it?'

Baruch indicated the way and followed me to the rear door, which he held open. The courtyard was larger than I might have expected. There was an opening in the whitewashed wall in which a tall gate had been fixed. The gate was not solid, so an intruder could have looked between the slats to see who was within; and there were large plants in pots in various places so it was not surprising that at first Isidore's parents had assumed he was concealed behind a pot.

'And the gate was closed when you came out here?'

'Yes, and before we let Isidore out. We always check, because we cannot see the gate from our back door, so whoever lets him out always comes here to see that the gate is properly closed, Master.'

Clearly the little boy could not have opened the gate himself, since the latch was about waist high to me.

'So how did the authorities think Isidore let himself out?' I demanded.

'They say he must have stood on something to reach up,' Pereyra explained, then mutely worked the latch and pulled the gate.

'But that's nonsense!' I remarked. 'The gate opens towards him. If he was standing on something, he would have to climb down and move it before he could get the door open. Surely that is beyond even the cleverest two-year-old?'

Pereyra shrugged. 'It is beyond a Portuguese two-year-old, but perhaps Dutch children are different.'

'Then how do they grow into the kind of stupid adults who would make such a suggestion?' I asked.

'That's a good question,' Pereyra replied. 'I suppose it's one of life's mysteries.'

CHAPTER SEVEN

Next, we visited the Pimentels.

Rachel Pimentel could not remember exactly what happened. Shmuel had been sitting there with his mother as she hemmed a blanket. The light inside the house was not good at that time of day, so she preferred to sit on the step and work there. Shmuel had been playing inside but had come to find her and sit with her. It was, said Rachel, about the eighth or ninth hour. She thought, but could not be sure, that she had hemmed one side and taken out the pins that had been holding the edges of the blanket together for hemming. The rough edge of the blanket was turned underneath, she explained, then fixed in place with a special style of stitch that gave a smooth, straight edge.

Having a handful of pins, she did not want to leave them where Shmuel might prick himself with them, so she took them inside to place in a bowl. She told Shmuel she would be straight back, but she could not have been gone as long as a minute.

Rachel's hands trembled as she spoke, and she moved her hand over her mouth, but it failed to stifle her tears. She shook her head, unable to complete her story.

'My wife came to find me,' said Saul Pimentel. 'She said she had searched the street and the house, but could not find Shmuel.'

'How far up the street did you search, mevrouw Pimentel?'

Rachel pointed to the bend in the road to one side and a crossroads to the other.

'Shmuel was small,' Saul explained. 'And he wasn't wearing anything on his feet. He couldn't have gone any further on his own. We concluded that someone must have taken him.'

'And no neighbours saw anything?' I asked.

'Many of them take a soneca after lunch.'

'Soneca?'

'A little sleep. It was the custom in our homeland and some have continued it here.'

'Is that generally known?'

Saul spread his hands in a gesture as if to say "Who knows?"

'Those who have business in this quarter know that it is often better to wait until three o'clock,' Pereyra commented.

'But you said your wife came to find you, mijnheer Pimentel, so you were at work?'

'Work? No, Master. I was at the synagogue.'

'Saul is one of our cantors,' said Pereyra. 'And a very good one too.'

'So it would be widely known that Saul would not be at home?'

Pereyra nodded. 'I suppose so. On Friday afternoon we have to prepare for the Sabbath. Since Sabbath begins at sunset, at that time of year preparations begin in the early afternoon.'

An idea suddenly presented itself to me. 'When were the other children taken?'

'The second day of November, 1683, and the seventh day of April, 1684.'

Working backwards from Christmas Day, 1683 I was soon able to calculate that the first child had also disappeared on a Friday; and since I knew that Easter Sunday in 1684 had been on 2nd April it was clear that the third child had also vanished on a Friday. This seemed very important to me. Of course, I had no idea why, but logically if children just wander off, they are as likely to do that on any day of the week. The idea that three very small children all spontaneously left their homes on the same day of the week seemed inherently unlikely to me.

As we journeyed to Daniel Morteira's house, I shared my discovery with Pereyra. If I had expected him to be impressed, I was soon disabused.

'Exactly, Master. I made that very point when I asked the Mayors to investigate. They argued that perhaps the parents were so occupied in their preparations for Sabbath that their attention was not on their children.'

'Does mijnheer Morteira have duties at the synagogue too?'

'Not formally. But Abraham is a devout man, often to be seen at afternoon prayers.'

'But the care of his child would surely fall on his wife? Does mevrouw Morteira do anything at the synagogue?'

Pereyra paused in his walk for a moment. 'Not in the synagogue. But Esther is one of those women who prepares a meal for our old people who cannot cook for themselves.'

'So it would be foreseeable to anyone who knew that that she would be in the kitchen?'

'I suppose so. But we can ask her ourselves, since we have arrived at their house.'

Once again Pereyra touched a little box on the doorpost and said a few words as we entered. There was no doubting that this was a house upon which tragedy had fallen, and quite recently. Mevrouw Morteira looked awful, lined and drawn. She could not have been an old woman but she appeared careworn and bowed under the great weight of life.

Her husband was a burly man with a large black beard. I would have thought he might have been thirty years old or so, and presumably his wife was the same or younger, though she did not look it. Abraham himself had dark circles under his eyes which blinked repeatedly as if smarting from the effects of a smoke I could not see.

Pereyra spoke to them in their own language. I had no idea what he was saying, but its tone was comforting. They looked at me at one point, from which I understood that he was explaining my purpose in being in their home.

Abraham addressed me in Dutch. It was accented, but not markedly so. 'We are grateful to you for having compassion on us. We just want to know what has happened to our Daniel. We pray that he is alive and well, but with each day that passes we know that the light of hope is fading.'

'I have no magical powers, mijnheer Morteira,' I replied, 'but what I can do, I will do. And I am sure that the Stadhouder will allow me to use all the resources at his disposal to help you.'

This may seem like a big promise, but I felt able to make it for a number of reasons.

First, because William was actually a compassionate man. [Marginal note: Van der Meer laughed when I dictated this. He claims it was a sneeze, but I know a giggle when I hear it. But William had a tender heart. Occasionally.]

Second, because he was determined to have a nation that was tolerant of religious differences and he was particularly keen for the Jews to settle here. They were devoted to him and could be relied upon to be loyal to him whatever their neighbours were up to, which William had good cause to appreciate. Not only that, they were very willing to lend him money, sometimes with little expectation of ever getting it back.

Third, and more cynically, once I had reported to him and he realised that the authorities in Amsterdam had not helped these families as they ought to have done, I had no doubt that he would spare no effort to rub in the difference between him and them. I could picture the anonymous broadsheets that would flood the streets declaring how William had protected Amsterdammers who had been let down badly by their elected officials.

Esther Morteira had turned her face away so that we could not see her crying, but I could hear her punctuated breathing as she choked back sobs.

'Perhaps you can tell me in as much detail as possible what happened on that Friday,' I said.

Abraham nodded. It was clear that his wife was going to have difficulty in contributing anything. 'Esther had been cooking and took meals to an old couple. The wife is now blind and her husband has difficulty in walking. Daniel was left with me while she was gone, so I took him into my workshop in his crib. He doesn't like it, but I can't let him crawl around in a room full of tools.' Abraham opened a door at the rear of the kitchen so we could see into his workshop. He seemed to be a metalworker of some kind. 'When Esther returned, I heard her come into the kitchen and carried the crib through for her. She had gone upstairs to put her shawl away. A few minutes later she came to scold me for letting Daniel come in the workshop when I should know he has to stay in his crib. I replied that he was in his crib, but she said he was not, and that was when we realised that he had been taken. Master, it cannot have been very long between Esther returning and her coming back downstairs.'

I was perplexed. 'But the city authorities claim he wandered off on his own?' I asked.

'They say one of us must have been mistaken and lifted him out because it is impossible that he was snatched from his crib with his parents both in the house. Then once he was on the floor he ran outside. Master, I swear we did not.'

'No oaths, Abraham!' Pereyra remarked.

I may not know much about investigating crime — who does? — but I know a bit about logical thinking, and something here was jarring.

It seems to me that there is some incongruity in asking witnesses what they saw and then telling them that they must be wrong. Why would the parents lie? I suppose some parents may feel remorse after neglecting their child who then comes to harm; as, for example, if they leave him unattended and he falls into a fireplace. In those circumstances I could imagine that they might construct some sequence of events which shifts blame away from them. They may say that they left him for no more than a minute when in fact it was five; that they were three paces away when actually it was twenty; that the child was warned but deliberately disobeyed them.

In this case, however, the parents did not know that their child had definitely been harmed. They seemed to have taken great care of the child, restricting him to a crib when he was in the workshop rather than risking injury. Even when he knew Esther had returned, Abraham had not taken Daniel out of the crib but had carried the child into the kitchen in the crib. These were not the actions of negligent or indifferent parents.

'Show me where you stand when you're working,' I requested.

Abraham walked back into the workshop and stood at a tall pedestal. It could hardly be called a table, since it was not much more than two handspans from side to side.

'I was here,' he said. 'The light is better on this side in the afternoon.'

'By your leave, may I stand there?'

Abraham moved to one side to allow me to take his place. It was true that in the afternoon the light would have been better here.

'You weren't at the synagogue?' I demanded.

'I should have been, I know,' he grimaced. 'But I needed to finish the work before the Sabbath started, and it had taken me longer than I expected.'

'What were you doing?'

'Repairing a salt cellar. It was in the shape of a boat but with a foot at each corner, and one of the feet had become bent underneath so it would not stand up. Unfortunately, the owner had tried to repair it himself by hammering the leg back in place, but the metal was quite thin and it pleated. I had to heat it gently and reshape it with a former, a sort of mould. It was quite intricate work. And because the metal was decorated, I could not heat it on the front side because I might lose the fine pattern if the metal melted.'

'So you must have been concentrating quite hard?'

'Yes, but I did not neglect my son! He was right there, not two strides from me, in the doorway.'

I followed his finger. There was not space in the workshop for the crib, so what Abraham actually meant was that he had taken the crib to the part of the kitchen just outside the workshop door, because that was the only part of the kitchen that he could see from where he stood.

'And where did you put the crib after Esther returned?'

Without a word Abraham strode forward and stepped three paces to his left. He then turned to the left and pointed to a spot another stride or so from him. 'There, so she could sit by the window and watch him.'

The place that he indicated was only a step or two from the back door.

'And the door was closed?'

'Definitely closed.'

Esther looked fretful and opened her mouth as if to speak but then thought better of it. Observing this, I addressed her directly. 'Did you want to say anything, Esther?'

The poor woman showed every sign of confusion, but finally blurted out her thought. 'Forgive me, I know a good wife does not contradict her husband, but Abraham is not quite right. He said I spoke to him a few minutes after I arrived, but it was not as long as that.'

'Minutes or seconds, does it matter?' Abraham snapped.

'Oh, yes, mijnheer Morteira, it matters a great deal,' I said, because an idea was beginning to form in my brain.

Abraham had a door to his workshop, presumably to keep noise and dust out of the house, but there were no other internal doors that I could see. One passed from one room to the next through a simple archway. Although the front and back doors were in line, the intermediate archway was shifted slightly. I suppose that prevented a draught blowing through the house, but it also disrupted the sightlines. From much of the kitchen you could not see the front door, and from the front hall you could not see much of the kitchen.

I thanked the Morteiras and assured them of my best efforts to solve the disappearance of their son, and we took our leave. Pringle had abandoned his attempts to have us ride in state everywhere and contented himself with following us along the road, intimidating the local population with his remaining eye and a drawn sword.

'Did you learn anything, Master?' Pereyra enquired.

'Certainly!' I replied. 'Probably. Perhaps.'

'Which is it?' Pereyra asked. 'Certainly, probably or perhaps?'

'I have an idea, but I need some time to formulate it in my head. And it only explains how the children were snatched, not who did it.'

'But you are convinced that they were, in fact, abducted?'

'Yes. I do not see how it can be otherwise.'

Pereyra seemed relieved. 'That, at least, is progress,' he replied.

'No children have been taken for a few weeks,' I noted.

Pereyra acknowledged the fact with a dip of his head. 'I persuaded the ma'amad that we must safeguard our children,' he explained.

'Who is the ma'amad?'

'I suppose you would call it the council of elders of the synagogue. They exercise some influence over our community as you might expect. Since Daniel Morteira was taken, families have been bringing their small children to the Esnoga on Fridays where they can be guarded by our men.'

'Doesn't that frighten the children?'

'We have told them they are having extra school lessons. Some would have been there anyway and there is plenty of space.'

'This Esnoga is a big building?'

'It is our synagogue.' Pereyra pointed to a roof visible between the buildings. 'There it is. Would you like to see it?'

'I would. I've never seen inside a synagogue.'

We threaded our way through the crowded streets, to the consternation of Pringle, who feared an assassin's dagger under every cloak, and found ourselves in front of a magnificent building. At the time of which I write, it had been completed less than a decade, and had the appearance of a large warehouse with seven windows on each level facing me. I had been in many less impressive churches.

The interior was simply beautiful. Magnificent chandeliers and wall sconces bore hundreds of candles, but even on this dull day the hall was filled with light. Tall pillars on each side supported a gallery in which, I was told, the women were accustomed to sit, the lower floor being reserved for men, it being the custom of the Jews to worship separately. Three barrel vaults ran the length of the building and the far end housed a splendid altar in which the holy things were stored. Despite it being an ordinary day there was some hubbub as men talked and made bargains, and in one corner small children sat cross-legged around an elderly teacher as he wrote letters on a slate. I think he was speaking Portuguese, which I do not have, but I could see from his writing that he was emphasising the importance of not confusing the letters resh and dalet, which can look very similar.

I suddenly realised that it was nearly four o'clock, and I must return to the negotiations; and while I should hate to be accused of gluttony, I had not had anything to eat since breakfast and I was by no means sure that I would be offered anything after the meeting. 'I must return to the town hall,' I announced, 'but I shall visit you again as soon as I can.'

'I am grateful,' said Pereyra. 'I knew that the Stadhouder would stand by us.'

In that case he knew more than I did. The Stadhouder, of course, knew nothing about their case, and while he was a fair man I do not know that three missing Jewish children would stand high on his list of priorities. If he interested himself at all, it would probably be as a means of drawing attention to the inadequacies of his opponents' actions in the matter. However, on any view of the facts it could not be denied that the Jews had a grievance. The idea that three children had somehow absented themselves from the family home and thrown

81

themselves in the nearest canal when one could not have opened the gate and another could not climb out of his crib would have been risible had it not had such serious consequences. These parents deserved to know what had happened to their children, and I fully intended to get to the bottom of the matter as soon as may be.

On the other hand, I had two other tasks that William had set me. I was required to persuade the Amsterdammers to pay their taxes in full, and to find out what the English exiles were plotting. Unusually, William was actually concerned about plots that were not aimed at him.

Pringle was waiting at the widest part of the street with my carriage. As I was entering it, the notion came to me to ask his opinion.

'I understand you are shortly to return to your own country, Captain,' I said.

'To England, Master, not my country.'

'I beg your pardon. May I ask, are your orders to help or hinder the Duke of Monmouth?'

Pringle looked mightily offended. 'I have taken an oath to the lawful King. I would not betray it.'

I felt the need to mollify him at once. 'I know that, Captain. That goes without saying. But I am more interested in whether anyone has attempted to seduce you from that allegiance.'

'I think, Master, that this is a discussion that you and I should reserve to another time and place,' said Pringle, and spurred his horse away.

I could not help but wonder what it was that he was reluctant to say in public.

CHAPTER EIGHT

When I arrived at the town hall, Hudde greeted me pleasantly enough.

'I hope you have passed a relaxing afternoon, Master.'

'On the contrary, I have been in the company of mijnheer Pereyra as we visited the families whose children have gone missing.'

Hudde at least had the grace not to repeat the disgraceful suggestion that the children were the authors of their own misfortune. 'And did you make progress?'

'Indeed I did. It is quite clear that the children were abducted.'

'I am sorry to hear it. We must have new enquiries made at once.'

'I beg that you will not trouble yourselves. I have the matter in hand on the Stadhouder's behalf.'

Hudde looked more than a little discomfited. He had the look of a man who had invited a guest to make himself thoroughly at home in his house and then discovered him in bed with his wife.

There was a very awkward silence.

'Master,' Hudde finally began, 'I would not have any misunderstanding between us. We bear no animosity towards the Stadhouder. We have no desire to see him replaced. We disagree on a matter of policy, it is true, but in other respects we are keen to maintain respectful and cordial relations with His Excellency.'

'Is that your personal view, or is it the opinion of you all?' I asked.

Hudde now looked as if the guest had moved to the bedroom of a favourite daughter. 'We are all loyal citizens,' he protested. 'But we are a collective leadership. We must all abide by the decisions of the mayors in council.'

That spoke volumes. Whatever his personal view, he considered himself bound by the majority view of the four mayors. Now, when a man says that it is usually because he was in the minority. Those in the majority prefer to give the impression that the decision was unanimous. I began to suspect that, with some skilled cultivation, mijnheer Hudde could be persuaded to ally himself with the Stadhouder. The trouble was that, when it came to cultivation, I did not have green fingers.

It also bore upon me that I had better write a letter that very night to the Stadhouder so that he knew what I was up to before the mayors contacted him, just in case he gave the game away by disclaiming any knowledge of my actions.

After all, he probably wanted to know what I was doing when it came to finding out what the English exiles were up to.

I just needed to find a way to dress up the word "nothing".

We walked through to the main hall where the mayors were sitting once more. This time they had placed themselves at a table, and cunningly ensured that from my seat I could not see all four of them at once.

I am a novice at diplomacy and statecraft, but I have sat through a number of meetings at the university, and I did what I once saw my friend Johannes Voet do in similar circumstances. He picked his chair up and moved it.

'That's better,' I remarked. 'I can see you all at once now.'

Huydecoper looked disgusted, so I suspect he was behind the manoeuvre in the first place.

The others seemed to defer to him, presumably because he had been a mayor longer than the rest, so nobody spoke until he had opened proceedings. He touched his fingers to his lips as if thinking hard, then launched into a speech that he must have prepared but which he intended to appear impromptu. 'We can, of course, fully support the Stadhouder in any preparations that he might make for a defensive war. We would not wish it to be thought otherwise. But his proposals are for an offensive engagement.'

'The Stadhouder believes that attack is the best form of defence,' I answered. I lifted a corner of my clerical gown to draw attention to it. 'Clearly I am not qualified to express an opinion on the military merits of such a view, but I observe that his martial record is extremely good.'

There are many reasons why nations win battles, and I am sure that the brilliance or otherwise of their commanders is only a partial cause. Having met some senior army generals, it surprises me that we have ever won anything, but I imagine the other side's officers must have been even dimmer. Come to think of it, entering a profession in which you are uncommonly likely to be killed is not an obvious mark of intelligence.

Out of the corner of my eye I could see Pringle sitting bolt upright by the window. He nodded his head slightly to show his approbation of my argument.

'But an attack is sure to precipitate retaliation, even from a country that had no immediate intention of attacking us,' Huydecoper argued.

'Then it would be wise to hit them so hard that they do not have the capacity to retaliate, would it not?' I rejoined.

I was beginning to enjoy this. I do like a good argument. I was hampered to some extent by not having a clue what I was talking about, but I reckoned that if I simply contradicted everything Huydecoper said I would be able to keep my end up.

'Bah!' snapped Huydecoper. I think that may be the only time I have heard someone say that in real life. As a contribution to a reasoned argument it was sadly lacking, so Geelvinck picked up the baton.

'The Stadhouder was elected by men,' he declared, 'and he can be unelected by them just as easily.'

Pringle sprang to his feet with his hand on the hilt of his sword, but thankfully Hudde intervened before he resolved the argument by killing one of the participants.

'Come, come!' said Hudde. 'There is no suggestion of that! Passions are running high, but let us all remain civilised men.' He waved to a nearby attendant and ordered him to bring wine. I am fairly sure that the attendant whispered that they had none in the building, so Hudde slipped him a coin and told him to get some somewhere, and be quick about it.

While we were waiting, Pringle marched across to me and leaned over to whisper in my ear. When he spoke, however, it was clear that he intended his comment to be overheard. 'As the Stadhouder's representative, you are authorised to summarily execute any traitors you may come across. I would, naturally, carry out any such order personally.'

It behoves a Christian to admit to his faults, and I have confessed before in my memoirs that I was not cut from the cloth of heroes, but even I put on airs when confronted by the reaction of the jumped-up chandler when he heard this. I did not know it at the time but Geelvinck had been ordered to assist William's defence of the country in 1672 by removing all the hay and peat that the French army might capture and use, and it was widely rumoured that not all of it found its way to the appointed warehouses. William had never been able to prove that it had been siphoned off, but he would have delighted in having a pretext to interrogate Geelvinck closely. If only William's torture master Beniamino had been at liberty to conduct the interrogation, we would soon have got at the truth, especially if he played the lute a little first to soften up his captive.

The attendant arrived with the wine and Hudde hastened to pour goblets for everyone — except, of course, Pringle and his men, who were not "anyone" and therefore did not count. I suddenly remembered that I had not eaten and I had suffered a previous bad experience when I had drunk wine on an empty stomach which I did not care to repeat, so I politely declined. This disconcerted Hudde, who seemed to interpret it as a reaction to the insult offered by Geelvinck.

'I fear that we have offended you, Master. That was not our intention.'

'I am sure it was not,' I replied. I was, in fact, not offended. Geelvinck had spoken, I suppose, only the literal truth. Of course, that would not have done him any good had William heard it, but I felt that a display of magnanimity was called for. 'Let us agree to overlook what was said,' I added, to the visible relief of Hudde, and, I think, Geelvinck, who had belatedly realised that he might have overstepped the mark. If he didn't, he was spurred to do so by Van Beuningen's poke in the ribs.

I eyed the goblet of wine and was sorely tempted to drain it, but I knew that drinking when I have not eaten does me no good. I was so hungry that even the thought of one of Albrecht's meals was beginning to appeal.

I am no stranger to fasting, but there is a difference between prayerful abstinence from food and just not being able to get any. The poor fast regularly, but it is not for any spiritual reason, and while no doubt it is counted to their credit, I think

Our Heavenly Father would much rather that men had the choice to eat or not.

I am sure that I am not the first person to remark on an oddity of the human senses which now presented itself. Having realised that I was hungry, I now could concentrate on nothing except where I might get something to eat. I caught a glimpse of Hudde's stockinged calf which reminded me strongly of a ham in a muslin net. Geelvinck's fingers called to mind plump little sausages. Huydecoper had launched into another of his dyspeptic rants, but I had no idea what he was saying because I was mentally comparing his head to a pudding — though a pudding, of course, would have talked more sense.

The meeting dribbled on for another three-quarters of an hour without any evident progress. Hudde assured me at least four times that they meant no disrespect to William of Orange who was undoubtedly the properly-elected Stadhouder ("For now", murmured Geelvinck) but that they were bound by their oaths as mayors to defend the rights and liberties of the city of Amsterdam.

'I am sure you must,' I replied at last. 'I would expect no less of men in your position.'

It was my good fortune that these four windbags were well able to maintain a conversation entirely unaided, with the result that I barely needed to say anything until the meeting ground to a halt shortly after half past six. We had all said all that could be said, or, in my case, decided not to say anything except the bare minimum.

As we rose from our chairs the oppressive thought bore down upon me that unless we reached some kind of agreement I could spend the rest of my life here, condemned to an endless cycle of inconclusive discussions and, more importantly, doing nothing to help the three Portuguese families who were expecting great things of me.

However I looked at the matter, I had too much to do. The first priority was to find something to eat. I could hardly go to Hudde's house, having missed dinner, and demand some supper. In fact, the idea was forming that being lodged with Hudde was not a good thing. It was making both of us uncomfortable.

I sought out Pringle and asked his help. 'I need to lodge somewhere else. Being mijnheer Hudde's guest is extremely awkward.'

'I know. That's why the Stadhouder told Hudde to host you. He hoped Hudde would give way to get you out of his house.'

I will admit to being gravely offended by this slur on my company. Well, perhaps not "gravely"; but definitely "slightly". 'I need something to eat anyway,' I grumbled.

'Leave it to me,' Pringle said, and approached Hudde, bowing deeply. 'Mijnheer, I hope you will forgive us, but I must bear Master Mercurius to an urgent meeting now. I will undertake that he will be returned to you by nine o'clock at the latest. My apologies for disturbing your household in this way.'

If anything, Hudde looked relieved that I would not be infesting his rooms for an hour or two, but then I saw a change in his countenance. He was wondering whom I was meeting at such short notice.

So, for that matter, was I.

Pringle's explanation was brisk and matter-of-fact. 'A subterfuge or stratagem, Master. Your appointment is with a beefsteak in the tavern that I have adopted as my quarters. But there is an ulterior motive.' Pringle looked about him for any sign of unfriendly ears. Given his monocular state, it was impossible for him to do this discreetly. 'You asked me whether anyone had attempted to seduce me from my allegiance to His Majesty.'

'I did. And you declined to answer.'

'I thought, perhaps, you would do me the honour of joining me for supper when I can unfold something of this to you. On the understanding, of course, that it is between us.'

I never like that last phrase. Suppose I had misjudged Pringle and he turned out to be a traitor? After all, he said he served the true King, but he had not said which particular King or would-be King that was. On the other hand, if I made such a promise and he proved to be speaking treason, nobody would criticise me for breaking my word. Except me, I suppose. In the end, I nodded mutely. That way, I could always claim that I never actually agreed to those terms; I just happened to have twitched.

We sat ourselves at a table in one corner of the tavern. I noticed that none of Pringle's men were there, and remarked on it.

'They are in a warehouse not far away. It's better like that. They can have their pleasures without feeling that an officer is watching their every move.'

The servant brought a flask of wine and some bread, so Pringle said no more until he was out of earshot.

'Here's a health to the King, the Stadhouder, you and me!' proclaimed Pringle.

'Yes!' I replied. 'Good health to all.'

Pringle lent forward. 'Don't turn round just yet, but I have an ulterior motive for bringing you here. Frankly there are better eating places, but none frequented by so many Englishmen. And one, at least, is known to me.'

Having been told not to turn and gawp, that, needless to say, is exactly what I did. 'Which one?'

'See you a lean gentleman, about fifty years old, narrow of face and with a sharply pointed nose? There, he is sitting facing us almost under the candles, with a book in his hand.'

The reader may imagine that it was not difficult to identify him given such a description. He was as close to the light as might be without risking the melted wax dripping on his head, and was reading intently, his large, dark eyes flicking rapidly along the lines of the page. At intervals he licked a finger to turn a leaf or groped blindly for his beaker of ale so as not to lose his place in the words. I admit that he seemed like a kindred spirit; how often might someone have spied me doing the very same thing in Steen's inn?

'Who is he?' I asked.

'That is the celebrated Mr Locke,' said Pringle. 'A noted philosopher and physician, lately arrived from England, and widely believed to have been one of the organisers of the Rye House plot.'

'I've heard of that,' I said.

'Yes,' said Pringle patiently, 'you're supposed to be investigating it; or, at least, finding out what the plotters are up to now.'

'Drinking beer and eating herring, by the looks of it,' I said.

'I doubt that is all they're doing,' Pringle observed. 'But if you don't ask, we'll never know.'

'I can't just walk over there and say "Oh, by the way, mijnheer Locke, are you plotting against the King of England?", can I?'

'No, and that is why you must be more cunning.'

'How?'

'I have no idea,' Pringle said, slurping from his goblet. 'But that's why I'm a soldier and you're a scholar.'

I thought hard. 'I must read something of his and engage him in conversation on the strength of it,' I said.

'Nice idea,' said Pringle, 'except that I doubt there's a bookseller within a week's walk that keeps any of his books.'

I thought hard for a while. 'Ah! I could mistake him for someone else and strike up a conversation as I apologise.'

Pringle pursed his lips. 'Possibly. Well, I leave that to you. He's doing no plotting tonight, being here alone except for his book.'

'You don't suppose he is here to lend his support to the Duke of Monmouth's escapade?'

'Monmouth was implicated in the Rye House plot, and Locke was alleged to be, but I don't see it.'

'No? Why?'

'Because Mr Locke has been strong in his insistence on a constitutional monarchy in parallel with a Parliament, such as was the original aim of our Civil Wars. He is an admirer of the Dutch system and sees the position of Stadhouder as the model for a modern king.'

I may have a reputation for honesty, but I had no intention of ever telling William that anyone thought he might serve in parallel with a parliament or that this was how the Dutch system works. So far as I could see, political stability here in the United Provinces depended on both the Stadhouder and the States-General believing that they had the upper hand, but neither of them wanting to press the point too much.

'Whereas,' continued Pringle, 'the Duke believes that he will one day be every bit as absolute a monarch as his father King Charles. He has no appetite for any curb on his bridle.'

I could see from this analysis that neither the Duke of Monmouth nor mijnheer Locke would find the other a congenial companion, but there have been plenty of plots in which the participants were not entirely of one mind. I am not well versed in English history, but I believe the opposition to the first King Charles consisted of those who wanted him executed and those who merely wished him deposed. They plotted together, but to different ends.

The arrival of our steaks put all thought of plotting out of my head. I said the fastest Grace I had ever pronounced before meat, and began to fill myself.

'How much do you know of my mission here?' I asked Pringle.

Pringle took his time to answer, pausing to take another draught of wine, and dabbing his mouth with a cloth. 'I know you are charged with investigating what the English exiles here are doing — obviously, since I mentioned Mr Locke to you — and I am also aware that you are tasked with getting these money-grubbing turncoats to hand over their taxes,' he said.

I nodded. That summed it up.

'Then, of course, you have enmeshed yourself in the matter of these Jewish children.'

'I cannot ignore the pleas of their anguished parents,' I answered.

'Of course not. Even Jewish ones feel pain. "If you prick us, do we not bleed?"'

I shook my head to clear my thoughts. 'What does that have to do with it? Who has been pricking you?'

'It's a quotation,' Pringle explained. 'From Shakespeare. In *The Merchant of Venice* there is a Jewish merchant called Shylock who lends money to a Christian against the security of a pound of his flesh, and when he is asked whether he actually intends to claim the bond he says he will, as an act of revenge, because Christians do not realise that Jews have the same feelings that they have.'

'I see,' I said, though I didn't.

'I don't remember it all, but Shylock says "If you prick us, do we not bleed? If you tickle us, do we not laugh?" Then a load of other stuff along the same lines that I don't honestly recall.'

'So it's a comedy?'

Pringle was confused. 'Why should it be a comedy?'

'That bit about tickling and laughing.'

'Perhaps it doesn't translate too well into Dutch. But it's certainly not a comedy.'

'And does the Jew take his pound of flesh?'

'No, because the court says he can take the flesh, but not one drop of blood, and he knows no way of taking one without the other.'

'So the bond was worthless?'

'Yes. That's the whole point. The Jew loses his money and can get nothing back.'

'So a Christian deceived him?'

'I think you're taking this a little too seriously.'

'Deception is a serious matter, Captain, no more to be practised on Jews than on Christians.'

'I have nothing against Jews myself,' Pringle said. 'In fact, there are some whose word I would take over any Christian, and certainly over that of the four grasping gold-buckets you are parleying with.'

'What do you make of them?' I asked.

I was genuinely interested to know because, frankly, keeping up a pretence of competence was occupying all my energies and I could not spare the effort to view them dispassionately.

Pringle called the pot-boy over and demanded that he refill our goblets. When he had gone again Pringle took another gulp of wine, rolled it over his tongue and swallowed it before beginning to speak.

'Hudde is the best of them. He doesn't like where they've put themselves. I think by nature he likes to be on good terms with all men. Disagreeing with the Stadhouder causes him some grief, but if you push him he will side with the others because he genuinely believes that's in the city's best interests. Van Beuningen is a windbag.'

'He isn't saying much to me.'

'He has wildly fluctuating humours, sometimes bright and cheerful, oft-times melancholy. It is his disposition and he'll not change. He is supposed to have tried to resign his post but then claimed it back. He'll swing the way the wind blows. If you get on top he'll switch to your side.'

'And Geelvinck?'

'Master, I've worked with many a mercenary and I see a mercenary's heart in him. His love is all for money. Persuade him he may lose all and he'll whimper back to his chests with some more locks and chains.'

'Then there's Huydecoper.'

'Aye, there's Huydecoper. He's the kingpin. Without Huydecoper, they'll crumble. He has an advocate's silver tongue and a serpent's slimy skin. He's the one you've got to turn.'

'And how will I do that?'

Pringle drained his goblet. 'If I knew that, Master, William would have given me the job and you could have stayed among your books. Come, drink up; we must take you back to mijnheer Hudde's house.'

We stood and began making our way to the door. Briefly Locke glanced up and our eyes met, before he decided I was insufficiently interesting and returned to his book.

Hudde was reading by the fire when I returned and invited me to sit opposite him.

'Some wine, perhaps?'

'Just a little, thank you. I've already had plenty.'

Hudde carefully tucked a length of ribbon in his book to keep his place before laying it aside. 'I fear, Master, that our discussions do not proceed well. At the risk of wearying you, is there nothing we can say that will assist you to understand our argument?'

'I think I understand it very well, mijnheer. I just don't accept it. And you will understand that my instructions from the Stadhouder leave me very little room for variation from his required outcome.'

Hudde looked as if he was in the grip of some painful affliction. At least twice he opened his mouth as if to speak, then thought better of it.

'I'm afraid my presence under your roof seems impolite since we are at odds. I will make arrangements to lodge elsewhere as soon as may be,' I said.

'No, no! I won't hear of it. You are my guest, and we are civilised men. We can disagree without being disagreeable,' Hudde answered, but while his mouth conveyed that message, his eyes suggested that his heart was not in it.

'You're very kind, and equally understanding.'

Hudde was gnawing a knuckle, deep in thought; unless, of course, he had missed his dinner too. 'How would it be,' he began, 'and of course I'm not saying that my colleagues will agree with this suggestion — they might very well not do so — but just as a proposition, let us say…' Then he stopped.

'Yes?' I prompted.

'Well, the Stadhouder wants money to finance a war against France that we do not want to have. But I wonder if earmarking might square this particular circle?'

He obviously thought I had some idea what he was talking about, and he was completely wrong about that.

'Earmarking, mijnheer?'

'Yes, earmarking. When a tax is devoted to a particular purpose rather than forming part of the general purse. If, for example, Amsterdam's money were to be devoted to, say, the payment of troops on the German border, that would mean it was not being used for a war against the French.'

'And William could then use the money he would have spent on the border to pay his troops going to France.'

'It's none of our business what the Stadhouder does with the money thus diverted, so long as we can say that he is not spending ours in this way.'

I began to understand. I did not like the idea, but at least I understood it now. 'I have no wish to appear argumentative,' I began, 'but does it make that much difference how it is used? Your money would still be financing a French war, however indirectly.'

Hudde looked at me as if I had just thrown manure over his favourite painting. 'Yes, Master,' he patiently explained as if to an imbecile, 'but it would not look that way. And appearances are everything in politics.'

I was feeling a certain amount of internal conflict. On the one hand, if I got the money for William I did not personally care if it was designated for buying sweetmeats. On the other hand, the philosophy lecturer inside me was itching to argue that it was the reality that mattered, not the appearance.

For example, if I were walking by the docks in Amsterdam and a sailor newly arrived from the East Indies were to ask me for some money so he could buy a whore or two, and I were to say "Here is a guilder, but you must use it to buy a bible," and he says that he will do so, surely I am abetting sin if common sense says that he is going straight to the nearest brothel where, I dare say, bibles are unlikely to be found?

'I will think about it,' I grudgingly conceded, 'but it becomes moot if your colleagues will not support you.'

'I will ask them first thing in the morning,' Hudde replied.

'In that case, perhaps it would be better if I absented myself for a while. I will look into mijnheer Pereyra's disappearing children for the morning, if that is agreeable.'

Hudde assented, and I bade him goodnight, retiring to my chamber to write a report for William. Kees was nowhere to be seen, which vexed me somewhat; not because I had anything I wanted him to do, but because for the first time in my life I had a servant and it seemed that he did whatever he wanted without reference to me. I am fairly certain that the master-servant relationship is not meant to work like that. [Van der Meer muttered something as he wrote that down. I did not quite catch it, but I can guess that it was unflattering to his master.]

CHAPTER NINE

Morning came, signalled by the battering of rain on the windows and the realisation that my bed was probably the warmest place I would encounter that day. When I reflect on how comfortable a good bed is, I sometimes wish I were an insomniac so I could experience its joy uninterrupted by unconsciousness. Of course, real insomniacs would tell me that there is no pleasure in it, and it must be annoying if one has a really comfortable bed and still cannot sleep. This is one of the drawbacks of a celibate life. There is nothing to do when you can't get to sleep at night.

Kees entered with some hot water for my shave.

'Where did you get to last night?' I asked.

'Me, Master? Why, I understood that you would not return until late, and you never have need of me at bedtime, so I went to bed.'

I could understand the logic behind that, but then a troubling consequential thought assailed me. 'Where?'

'I beg pardon, Master?'

'Where did you go to bed?'

Kees did not appear to understand that simple question, so I elaborated somewhat.

'You usually sleep at the foot of my bed, but unless I miss my guess you were not there when I retired last night. I think I would have noticed a lump like you on the floor — not to mention that there was a welcome absence of snoring.'

'I don't snore, Master! Do I?'

'Not snore, perhaps,' I conceded. 'It's more like a pig snuffling.'

'Sorry,' he said.

Silence ensued until I broke it. 'So I repeat, where did you sleep?'

'In the kitchen, Master.'

That would not be unreasonable. The kitchen was the warmest place in the house at night; yet something told me that there was more to be discovered.

'This would not have anything to do with mijnheer Hudde's little dark-haired maid, would it?'

'Master! The very thought!'

'Because if I thought you were defiling a young virgin, I…'

'Virgin? Marietta — a virgin?' he exclaimed.

'She is young and unmarried,' I replied. 'And therefore surely virtuous.'

'We are talking about Marietta who lays the breakfast?' Kees asked. 'There aren't two Mariettas?'

'Not that I know of. Nor do I know the girl's name, but you clearly do.'

'We've been introduced,' he admitted.

'Well, see that your acquaintance becomes no more intimate. I would not want to have to answer for your conduct to her angry mistress.'

'You have nothing to worry about, Master,' Kees assured me.

I am fairly sure that his fingers were crossed behind his back.

While Hudde attempted to persuade his colleagues to accept his proposal, I went to Pereyra's warehouse to discuss what further steps we might take. Pereyra was once again in his shirt sleeves as he inspected the contents of various kegs and chests. Producing a piece of chalk from his coat pocket he marked a cross on one such barrel.

'My compliments to the master of the *Zeewolf*, but he cannot expect me to accept that slush. Seawater has seeped in. I will adjust the payment accordingly.'

The clerk marked the manifest accordingly without attempting to argue.

'Forgive me, Master,' Pereyra said. 'I must complete my inspection so that the ship can sail on the evening tide. I may be an hour or so.'

'That is no problem, mijnheer,' I replied. 'I can find my own way to the relevant streets and make the observations I need on my own. I will return in due course.'

We bowed formally, but not flamboyantly, and each turned to our task. I could see the synagogue roof, so all I needed to do was to make my way in that direction and navigate from there.

People sometimes talk about "the Jewish Quarter" of Amsterdam. There is certainly a district where Jews have congregated, but it is not theirs exclusively, and Christians mingled with them without hindrance. I was told, for example, that the painter Rembrandt lived here for a while before his money troubles got the better of him. Nevertheless, it surprised me a little to see a monk or friar crossing the road in front of me. He was a young man, as shown by the nimble way in which he swerved between the horses and carts, and evidently in a hurry. Running in a habit is not easy, and I feared that he would take a tumble if he did not slow down. In the event he was obliged to stop because there was no gap in the crowd on the pavement, so he had to push his way gently through the throng. When I reached the corner of the street, I glanced the way that he had gone and saw him enter at the door of a house about a block further back.

The grey habit marked him out as a Franciscan, which surprised me more than a little. The laws that imposed restrictions on Catholics were not often enforced, but they still existed, and Catholics had learned discretion as the price of being able to worship privately unmolested; to walk through the streets openly wearing a religious habit seemed foolhardy to me, but my interest had been pricked. One way by which the regulations were skirted was that Catholic churches were concealed inside or behind ordinary houses. Could the building he had just entered be one of these? If so, it would be pleasant to spend a few minutes on my knees seeking the assistance of the Almighty though, on any reading of the past record, the Almighty seemed supremely indifferent to my enquiries and had declined to involve himself despite frequent requests.

As I expected, the house door was not locked, and I was able to walk into a passageway which led into a small garden or courtyard with another door to each side. I had no idea which way my friar had gone, but since the building on my left fronted the road it seemed more likely that the church, if any, would be in that to my right.

On the other hand, I could be entirely wrong, and it might be a private house. Perhaps the friar was simply running an errand; fetching some medicine for a sick man, for example. Thus uncertain, I stood for a moment in thought until I sensed, rather than saw, some movement at a window. Surely that was a grey habit? I began to walk towards the door, but it opened abruptly and a stocky figure with a tonsure emerged.

'May I help you?' he enquired pleasantly.

'I understood there was a concealed Roman Catholic church nearby,' I replied boldly. 'Is this it?'

The priest opened his arms wide as if about to pronounce "Dominus tecum", though I think in this case it was to prevent my access. 'We want no trouble, dominie,' he said.

I had forgotten that I was dressed as a Reformed minister, so it is not surprising that he viewed me with some suspicion. 'Neither shall you have any, Father,' I replied.

I toyed with disclosing my little secret to him, but on balance it seemed imprudent to do so. My original idea was thwarted anyway, because a Reformed minister praying in a Catholic church was bound to attract some notice, but if I discovered what manner of building this was I might return later in civilian clothes, if I had remembered to bring any.

'I am Cornelis de Vroom, a priest here. People will tell you that we obey all the restrictions placed upon us. We have no interest in arousing suspicion of our faith or our motives.'

'Of course. I am Master Mercurius of the University of Leiden. I am here at the command of the Stadhouder.'

De Vroom swallowed hard. I do not know what he anticipated next, but whatever I was about to say he was sure that it would not be to his liking. 'We are his loyal subjects,' he said unconvincingly.

'Then I am sure you will wish to afford me every assistance in your power,' I said. I did not actually believe that, but it seemed to me to trap him nicely into helping me. 'I am investigating the disappearance of three Portuguese children from this district,' I told him. 'Are you able to throw any light on this?'

'Three local children?' he said. 'I had not heard. But I am afraid I know nothing that can help you. There are no children here. You are welcome to search the building if you must.'

I am sure that the offer would not have been made if he thought there was the remotest chance that I would find something, which hinted strongly at his innocence; on the other hand, perhaps he was a child murderer but competent enough to ensure that all traces of the children had been destroyed.

Although I am the first to admit that I am a poor judge of character, he seemed an honest man to me. Believe me, I have met some wicked priests in my life, and they were not that difficult to pick out. I bring to mind one in Germany who had four mistresses whom he invited simultaneously to his chamber where he would…

Never mind. That has nothing to do with this story. [Van der Meer put down his pen in the hope that I could be induced to tell him the full tale in private. I will not do so. For a start, it occurs to me that I don't actually know what he did with the four young women except that his housekeeper told me that they got through an awful lot of walnuts while they were doing it.]

'That will not be necessary,' I replied. 'I am pleased that I will be able to tell the Stadhouder that you were co-operative.'

De Vroom relaxed. 'Since you are here, may I offer you a little refreshment?'

'That is very kind of you, but I am afraid I have very little time at present. Perhaps another time?'

'Of course. Just announce yourself at that door and I will be glad to receive you,' he said, indicating a door in the corner that presumably led to the priests' quarters.

We parted on polite terms and I made my way back to the street. Of course, I knew several concealed churches in Leiden, Delft and such places, but it still surprised me to have found one here, and one of such dimensions. So far as I could tell it consisted of two houses that had been conjoined but which stood in the centre of a block with no street access directly to the church. Who could have imagined that this church was even here?

It gave me pause. What else was I not seeing that was as plain as the nose on your face?

I walked along the street once more, pausing at the doorstep where Shmuel Pimentel had been sitting. It was incomprehensible. How could a boy less than three years old have put such a distance between himself and his parents that he could not be found although the alarm had been raised immediately? Surely he must have been abducted in a carriage; but that could hardly be true of the others, for Isidore had been in a courtyard that opened onto a narrow lane, while Daniel had been snatched through the back door of his house for which the same problem obtained, because no carriage could have navigated the lane behind in safety. Even if a reckless driver had attempted it, the accumulated refuse would have impeded their flight afterwards.

I followed the route from the Pimentels' house to the home of the Morteiras as I had the other day, but then I realised that I had entered the house through the front door. What I really needed to see was the back door. But how should I find it?

I walked around the block a couple of times. Although I have spoken of a lane, these houses did not have straightforward access to the rear. Instead there seemed to be a couple of entries which snaked around the back of a few houses into a common area that lay at the rear of them, but these alleyways did not always connect. In some cases one would have to retrace one's steps to leave by the way one had entered, as I discovered when I tried to gain the rear entrance of the Morteiras' house, because on my first attempt I came upon a wall that denied me access. I walked round to the next opening between the houses and tried again. The path forked at one point, so I chose to take the left branch and was rewarded with arrival at their rear gate. Entry was blocked by something heavy placed behind the wooden gate, but through a knothole I could see that it was only a few steps to the back door. Since the weather was fine the door was open, and Esther Morteira was sitting in the doorway rubbing her washing with soap.

I retraced my steps, and then thought to return to the Pimentel dwelling. It took me a moment to gain my bearings, whereupon I realised that I could simply cross the road from the end of the alleyway, walk to the corner, and the house would be not a hundred paces away, a considerably shorter distance than I had thought. I was still standing deep in thought when mijnheer Pereyra found me.

'You look puzzled, Master.'

'I am. How did you find me in this knot of streets and lanes?'

Pereyra laughed gently. 'It's not so difficult. People may not know who Master Mercurius is, but they never miss a stranger. I asked if anyone had seen a Reformed minister and several people told me exactly where you were and where you had been.'

'Did they indeed?' I did not like the thought of being spied upon.

'Yes, they told me you had been to the Moses and Aaron Church.'

'Is that the secret Catholic church?'

'That's right.'

'It's an odd place to establish a church, isn't it? There cannot be many Catholics nearby.'

'There aren't, but they travel from other parts of Amsterdam, I believe. And it isn't so strange when you think about it. If you built a Catholic church in a Protestant neighbourhood there would be friction, claim and counter-claim, and, perhaps, too much scrutiny of what the Catholics were doing. Here they escape that. They know that Jews are unlikely to inform on them, not because we are a superior people, but because we have no particular dislike for them.'

I had not thought of that. The Jews would not care very much what the Catholics did in their midst so long as they did not interfere with each others' freedoms. But my interest was piqued. 'How do your people view the controversy between the Catholic and Reformed churches?' I asked.

'What controversy?' Pereyra replied.

'You don't know?'

'Whatever differences you have, they pass us by,' he replied. 'I hear little snippets, of course; that you disagree about this or that, but since we think you're both wrong we do not exercise ourselves over it. I mean no offence,' he added quickly.

'I take none.'

'Plainly you are a learned man, Master. You work at the celebrated University of Leiden, and I see by your dress that you are some kind of minister. But how you differ from Father de Vroom at the Moses and Aaron Church, I do not know.'

Not by as much as I pretend, I thought, but decided to hold my counsel for the moment. Nothing would be gained by self-disclosure, and it would put me in mijnheer Pereyra's power. I doubt that William would imprison me, though I expect that he would be more worried by my secrecy than by the fact that I was a Catholic; but the university would discharge me and, if the truth be told, there is not much that I can do other than being a university lecturer. It is all I have ever done. Remove me from that and I do not know how I would live. There is not much work for a door-to-door moral philosopher.

The Catholic Church might have found me something, but I would probably have had to move to Flanders, where my bishop was situated; a thought which recalled to mind that I still had to make some kind of arrangement to visit him or at least explain why I could not go. At least his agents were unlikely to track me all the way to Amsterdam, though if one were indiscreet in Leiden it could cause me a deal of worry or discomfort.

'Do you know Father De Vroom?' I asked.

'Not personally, but he is frequently seen about the district. You will know that my people fled Spain and Portugal because of persecution by the Catholic Church, so one might expect us to view him with suspicion, but he seems an honest man and has done much to restore good relations. That is why I say that we do not resent the secret church here. Things might be different with another priest.'

'I see.'

'I know that he has been trying to persuade his neighbours to sell their properties to him so that he can expand his church. He seems to have quite a store of money to hand.'

'And would they sell to a Christian?'

Pereyra smiled. 'Master, some of my compatriots would sell their grandmothers if there was profit in it.'

I do not think I was intended to take that literally. In any case, I cannot think why a man would want more grandmothers than he already has. I had recently lost mine, who was irreplaceable in my life, though at least I now did not have to explain why I had not married every time I visited her.

'You told me that there had been no further abductions, mijnheer. Have there been any attempts?'

'Not that I know of.'

'You see,' I mused, 'I can understand why the kidnappings might suddenly start, if, for example, someone moved into this district. But it is much harder to explain why they should stop just as suddenly.'

'Surely the measures we have taken have prevented more.'

'I am sure that the measures have been effective, but you miss my point. In around five months someone took three children. Such repeated crimes betoken someone who acts under the strongest compulsion. He needs to seize little children. He has taken considerable risks to snatch these three, and the risks were increasing. The first taken from a courtyard, the second from the very doorstep of the house, the third from inside the house; this indicates a man acting under the influence of a very strong and wicked drive.'

'I understand your point,' Pereyra commented.

'The hand of the devil himself may be in this.'

Pereyra shook his head. 'We do not believe in a devil such as you do, Master. To us, Satan can do only what God permits, as when he tested Job. But each of us has our own Satan, our own nature impelling us towards unrighteousness.'

'Well, we are not so far apart, mijnheer Pereyra. I do not mean that the devil himself came to Amsterdam and stole your little ones. Rather, that someone who is unable to resist his promptings is doing this. Now, I cannot believe that the promptings have ceased, which is why I asked if there had been any unsuccessful attempts. He may not succeed now, but it seems unlikely to me that he is not trying.'

Pereyra nodded gravely. 'I will ensure that we do not relax our vigilance.'

'I think that would be wise,' I said. 'Until I understand how the villain thinks, I cannot suggest any better ideas.'

We walked along together.

'I had not realised how close together the three abduction sites are,' I said.

'This is a small neighbourhood,' said Pereyra. 'Nowhere is very far from anywhere else, if you know the shortest route.'

'I begin to think our kidnapper does,' I replied.

Pereyra stopped walking. His face showed evidence of some great pain.

'Are you all right?' I asked.

'If he knows our neighbourhood, he may be one of us,' he whispered. 'It is almost beyond belief that one of our people would do this to others in our community.' Pereyra appeared very shaken.

'I do not say it is so,' I replied, 'but we must prepare ourselves for this possibility.'

Pereyra composed himself and looked at me intently. 'If it is so, then it is so, Master. We do not want any favours for one of our own. Such wickedness must be punished severely.'

'If the children have been killed, the murderer will die for it.'

Pereyra winced, but nodded. 'We are taught that a death sentence can only be justified if someone is caught in the act by unimpeachable witnesses. It is better that a thousand guilty men go free than that one innocent be deprived of life.'

'And do you agree?' I asked.

'I follow the teachings of wise men, though this evil among us tests my fidelity to their word.'

I did not like to say that I agreed with the teaching. I had never liked the idea that a man might hang because of my work. At that stage of my life three men had paid the ultimate penalty for crimes that I had detected, and from time to time I woke suddenly at night in the grip of a dream that I was being judged for having done wrong in these matters. When, as I hope, I come face to face with God, will He hold me blameless for my part in depriving murderers of their lives? I hope so, but until it happens, I cannot be sure.

CHAPTER TEN

Pringle was furious. 'You must not slip away like that, Master!' he bellowed. 'I cannot guarantee your safety if I do not know where you are.'

'I told you I was going to the Jewish district,' I complained.

'Yes, but you didn't say that you were going to venture out on your own instead of waiting for your armed escort.'

'As you have pointed out,' I remarked with a certain amount of asperity, 'your orders do not extend to my private investigation into the abduction of the children.'

'Indeed. But they do cover assisting you to bring your state business to a successful conclusion, which will be rather difficult if you are lying in a ditch with your throat cut.'

I felt my neck gingerly. I did not like the sound of that.

'Can you imagine what sort of welcome I will receive at The Hague if I return with your body in a cart? It doesn't bear thinking about.'

He was right there. If he didn't like thinking about it, you can imagine how I felt on the matter.

'I accept your reproof,' I declared submissively. 'I won't do it again.'

Pringle's anger subsided somewhat. 'I apologise for my sharpness,' he mumbled. 'It's just that you make it hard for me to do my job.'

'As I said, I accept your reproof. I am grateful for the assistance you are giving me.'

Pringle was now entirely mollified. 'I have sent one of my best men to The Hague with your report,' he said. 'Given that the weather is quite good, and assuming he is able to change his horse, he should arrive sometime today, and he has orders to bring back any reply the Stadhouder chooses to entrust to him.'

'Thank you,' I said. 'That is very convenient.'

I meant it. Any other method of sending a letter across the country would have been much slower, if it got there at all. The only thing I would have had in my favour would have been that it was addressed to His Excellency the Stadhouder, and it would be a brave man who interfered with correspondence to him; or, I suppose, an illiterate one.

'The meeting of the mayors has broken up,' Pringle remarked.

'Do you have any idea how it went?'

'To judge by the language being used and the volume of the voices, I think it unlikely that they came to a meeting of minds,' sighed Pringle.

'And you were able to hear this — how?'

'With a couple of men and a long ladder. And we bribed one of the servants to leave a window slightly open. Remarkably cheaply, actually. I would have expected him to ask for more, which suggests that they are very poorly paid. That's always good to know, Master. Bribery is much more economical when men have a low estimation of their own value.'

'I'm not sure that I approve of such methods,' I said.

'Oh, Master!' Pringle exclaimed. 'If you imprisoned everyone who had given or received a bribe, our government would be in the hands of about three men. And they would be the ones too stupid to ask for a bribe.'

'I am shocked!'

'I understand that you are a minister of the church,' Pringle answered, frowning to show his perplexity, 'but surely bribery is not entirely unknown in ecclesiastical circles?'

That was a tricky one. The Roman Catholic Church had used and abused bribery for a long time. It was a standard method of acquiring a bishopric, despite the attempts of some well-meaning Popes to put a stop to the practice by refusing such bribes; which only meant that they were given to the Popes' secretaries instead. The Reformed Church was much less susceptible to malpractices of this type, largely because it kept its ministers too poor to pay much in the way of bribes. And even if we had the money, there were no "top jobs" to be had because each parish chooses its own minister and we don't have bishops. Besides, you can't bribe everyone in a parish.

'Have you ever received a bribe, Captain?' I asked.

'Certainly not.'

'I am pleased to hear it.'

'It would be death to my profession. When you're a mercenary, your employer has to know that his money has bought your entire support. You can't be seen to be sub-contracting to others. I have, of course, received the occasional unsolicited gift, but it would be impolite to refuse those.'

'Just so I know where I stand, if someone offered you a hundred gold pieces to kill me, what would you say?'

'I would wonder why he thought your life was worth so much, but since he does, I would ask for a little more. He would obviously be keen to be rid of you, so it would not surprise me if I could bargain for a higher fee.'

'That's not exactly reassuring,' I remarked.

'Then I would come to you, because whatever your life is worth to him, it will be worth more to you.'

I was very glad I had kept out of politics. I plainly had no head for it.

'But rest easy, Master. No amount of gold would compensate for having to explain myself to the Stadhouder, for you are his man. He would take it very unkindly if someone were to kill you. Which is why I beg that you will not go off on frolics of your own.'

'Very well,' I said. 'Where are we going now?'

'Wherever you wish, Master. You're the Stadhouder's emissary, not me. But if you want some dinner, I suggest we return to the inn we visited the other day. You might be able to strike up a conversation with that Englishman.'

I allowed myself to be persuaded and clambered aboard the waiting carriage. To my surprise I noticed Kees approach Pringle, who pointed somewhere and sent Kees on his way. I suppose Kees had been sent ahead to ensure that a suitable table was reserved for us, but I was unsure why Pringle sent Kees instead of one of his own men. After all, I might have wanted Kees for something. I have no idea what, because I am not used to having a personal servant, but it's the principle of the thing.

We arrived at the inn and sat ourselves at the same table as before. Locke was not there.

'Were your enquiries fruitful, Master?' asked Pringle.

'I took a small step forward, I think. It became clear that the sites of the abductions are much closer together than I had imagined. But the overriding impression was that whoever did this knows his way around the district.'

'Or her way.'

'Her way?'

'You're speaking as if the kidnapper must be a male. I merely note that women are just as likely to steal a child, if not more so. For a start, they are better able to care for a small infant.'

I considered what Pringle had said. 'Let us hope that you are right, because that implies that the intention was to keep the child rather than kill it. I take comfort from the fact that no bodies have been found.'

'I wouldn't take too much, Master. It would be an easy matter to put a baby in a sack with a few rocks and ensure that he did not surface from a canal.'

I blanched. Who could imagine such wickedness? 'But who could hate little children so much that he kills three of them?'

'Maybe he doesn't,' Pringle shrugged. 'Maybe he hates the parents. Or he hates Jews.'

'But why kill children? Surely if you hate Jews you kill adult Jews?'

'Kill an adult Jew and there is one less Jew. Kill a few Jewish children and there will be a dozen or so fewer Jews in a generation.'

My appetite was rapidly waning. I know that I have led a sheltered life, but I have never encountered a degree of hatred of an entire people such that its proponents would harm children.

'Why do you suppose that the abductor knows the area?' Pringle asked.

'The Morteira boy was stolen through the back door, but it is not easy to find that rear entrance. You'd need to know which passageway must be taken. And the kidnapper could not be idly strolling past, for that pathway is a dead end. It leads nowhere else.'

Pringle nodded his agreement. 'That much I can follow. It tells us also that these are not opportunistic abductions. The perpetrator followed that alleyway for a purpose, and the purpose must have been to snatch a child. The question then becomes — that child, or any child?'

'Surely that's obvious. Given that there was probably only one option, the villain must have planned to take Daniel Morteira.'

'You misunderstand me. It's true that having got there he had only one choice. What I was asking is whether the intention from the outset was to snatch the individual children taken, or whether any child would have done.'

Those who have followed my memoirs from their debut will recall that in my very first mystery three children went missing, but the man responsible was actually looking for a particular child. Could that be true here?

This was patently a matter of the highest importance, so I concentrated on that very hard for a few minutes, during which I seemed to have absent-mindedly drunk two more goblets of wine while Pringle devoted his attention to a ragout of hare.

Having no images of the infants I could not say definitively that they could not be mistaken for one another, but on the face of it one would have thought it unlikely because Shmuel was twice the age of Daniel. Was it suggestive that they were all boys, I wondered? 'How do they know?'

'How do they know what, Master?'

I have a very bad habit of occasionally voicing my thoughts aloud. I have no idea why I do it and I wish I could stop, but it seems to be ingrained in me. 'I'm sorry, Captain. I was pondering whether the kidnapper is deliberately going for boys. If he is selecting at random, I wonder what the chances are that he would pick three boys?'

If I had been in Leiden I could have asked Master Hubertus, who knew all kinds of mathematical jiggery-pokery and could probably tell me the answer, provided I managed to keep his mind on it for long enough. Hubertus was brilliant but scatter-brained. In any case, he was not here, and it was not worth writing to him for an answer. Whatever it was, I thought the chances must be quite remote.

'Any gambler can tell you it's one in eight,' Pringle declared, surprising me considerably given that he did not have any mathematical training.

'How so?' I asked sceptically.

'Well, it's the same as three coin tosses, isn't it? If half the babies are boys and half are girls, that's like saying what are the odds that a man will toss three heads in succession.'

I could see that. I am not particularly gifted mathematically and I do not gamble, but that much I could understand.

'So,' continued Pringle, 'if you toss a coin twice, you can get a head followed by a tail, or a tail followed by a head, or two heads or two tails. There are four equally likely options, so the odds must be one in four that you will get two heads.'

'Ye-es,' I agreed. If I sounded dubious, it was only because I was doubtful that a soldier could know any mathematics. Gamblers, of course, are the best mathematicians around, because they are prepared to spend a lot of time on working these things out.

'Then,' Pringle concluded, 'when you then add a third toss you have eight possibilities, because each of the four I listed can be combined with either a head or a tail. Thus the chances of three heads are one in eight.'

I badly wanted to go and write this down before I forgot it, but I could not fault his logic. 'It sounds quite unlikely that the children are being chosen at random, then,' I said. 'Whoever he is, he wants boys.'

'So it would seem. If a fourth child disappears and it is another boy, we would feel more secure in our supposition, of course.'

'Let us pray that it does not come to that.'

'Amen, Master. But what were you thinking when you spoke aloud earlier?'

'I was wondering how he knew that these three children were little boys. After all, at that age boys and girls are dressed similarly. Yet our man has taken three boys.'

'Presumably he didn't rely on appearance. He knew those children were boys.'

'More evidence that he knows the neighbourhood. He must be a local man.'

'But then we face another question, Master. Where are the children now, because it sounds as if mijnheer Pereyra and the synagogue authorities have searched diligently through those streets for them without success?'

'The place is riddled with canals, Captain. The children could be on a barge and away from the district within minutes.'

Pringle took a long draught and thought for a moment. 'That is true of the first child, but for the third child he had to retrace his steps along a tortuous alleyway and the second child's home is about as far from water as any in Amsterdam.'

'Yes, but none are very far.'

'We must ask mijnheer Pereyra whether they searched any barges. Meanwhile, Master, may I draw your attention to the fact that Locke has arrived and is sitting by himself. This would be a good time to introduce yourself.'

'With what object?'

'Either you feign interest in his wicked plans and hope that he takes you into his confidence, or you tell him that you are the Stadhouder's representative and warn him to behave himself while he is a guest in your country. The choice is yours. I don't think the Stadhouder will care how you do it, so long as you ensure that there is no English plotting here that might cause him embarrassment.'

I took another goblet of wine while I considered my best approach.

'I'll tell you what,' said Pringle, observing my caution in the matter. 'How about you tell him that plotting against King Charles will not be tolerated and if he intends to do it he can depart the country at once? Then when he leaves the inn I can get a couple of my men to beat the living daylights out of him to underline the message.'

While this approach was superficially attractive, I could not condone the use of violence. Apart from any other consideration, it is my experience that those who are beaten tend to retaliate by beating someone on the other side, and given a choice between trying to thrash a soldier or a lecturer in moral philosophy, the wise man will not choose the soldier.

I drained my goblet to strengthen my resolve. 'I'll do it now,' I said. 'Perhaps you would stand ready to intervene if he turns nasty.'

'He's a philosopher,' Pringle protested. 'Is he likely to turn nasty?'

'I know philosophers,' I said. 'Some of them can be quite brutal when they're crossed.' I confess that I have never known a philosophical dispute descend into physical violence, but they can become very heated and strong words may be used.

I walked over to the table where Locke was sitting and indicated the empty stool opposite. 'May I have a few words with you, mijnheer Locke?' I asked.

Locke looked up. It was clear that my interruption of his reading was unwelcome, a sentiment with which I was only too familiar, but after a moment or two he deigned to reply. 'It is a public place and I do not determine who sits where, mijnheer; but you have the advantage of me, for you know my name yet I do not believe that you have been introduced to me.'

'That is true, mijnheer. I am Master Mercurius of the University of Leiden. However, I am here in Amsterdam as the representative of the Stadhouder, His Excellency William of Orange.'

'Then I take this to be some species of official business?' Locke suggested.

'Yes, but I hope that we may have some conversation without reserve or formality.'

'I hope so too, but on what subject, if I may be so bold?'

'On your plans, mijnheer. His Excellency takes an interest in English affairs, being closely connected to the Royal Family there. At the same time, it is the policy of our land to admit all of a peaceable disposition without any religious or political prejudice. Occasionally these two interests clash to some extent.'

Despite my flowery circumlocutions, Locke was intelligent enough to divine what I was driving at. 'You are worried that I may be planning the overthrow of King Charles?'

'That is one concern, certainly.'

'And since the Stadhouder is married to the woman second in line to the English crown, he is worried that I may be aiming at the removal of the Stuart family from the throne.'

'Something like that.'

Locke took a pull at his beer. 'So if I plotted against Charles in order to put his brother James on the throne, presumably William would like that, since it would move his wife one step nearer the crown?'

That was a difficult one to argue against, but I did not want Locke to think that William acted only out of self-interest. 'I believe my master is keen not to allow anything that suggests that rulers in any nation can be removed by a faction.'

'He would be,' Locke agreed. 'Since you have been frank with me, permit me to return the compliment.'

I obviously could not get the hang of diplomacy, because I thought I had been anything but frank. I had tried to cloak my meaning so that my words could mean anything or nothing.

'It is true that I have not been enamoured of His Majesty the King, but this is not directed at his person or, indeed, his personal qualities. I believe, Master, that a man should have a stake in the government of his nation; that, in short, he cannot be considered as bound to any government in which he has had no voice. I admire the Dutch system in which the Dutch people have freely placed themselves under the Stadhouder who has the powers of a king but has been selected by the people and has their consent and support.'

If Locke believed this, I can only say that he had clearly not been in our lands for very long and had much to learn, but I held my peace.

'I live in hope that one day my own land will be as enlightened,' Locke continued. 'I have no animosity towards His Majesty, but I believe that power is derived from the people, and that the people's representatives are the Commons in Parliament. It follows that a King must be subject to the will of Parliament; in short, I argue for a constitutional monarchy. If Charles will give us that, I will rejoice and wave my hat while offering him three cheers. But experience over nearly a quarter of a century has shown us that this is far from Charles's mind; and his brother is, if anything, even less fettered by such principles. There are things that Charles could do, but does not do, because he is a sensible man who does not wish to provoke others. James recognises no such constraints. Consider, then, Master, where we are come to. It is unlikely that Charles will agree to reform, but if we remove him to place James in charge, reform is even less likely; and James, of course, is a notorious Roman Catholic who wishes to ally us with France, a move that would be unpopular in the country. Why would I seek to remove Charles when the real danger lies in his successor?'

'There may be alternative successors available,' I hinted.

'I think you may be referring to the Duke of Monmouth. Really, mijnheer, I marvel that the Stadhouder tolerates his presence here, since it must surely provoke King Charles to know that one who covets his throne is given sanctuary in the United Provinces.'

'I have not heard that the Duke proposes to move against King Charles,' I said.

'You believe, as do I, that he intends to intervene when King Charles dies to prevent James's accession to the throne, and is readying himself to make his play when that comes to pass. Well, that may be so. But if he does that and succeeds, Princess Mary's claim may as well be thrown to the wind, because she will have been displaced and the Duke is a lusty young gentleman who has already fathered many children.'

That was true. He had eight or nine already, and his wife was young enough to have several more. If the Duke achieved the thrones of England and Scotland, Mary would no longer have a real claim.

'I do not believe, mijnheer, that the Duke of Monmouth is any more likely to grant us the political changes that we wish to see,' Locke continued. 'Whereas I judge that your master and the Princess may be willing to do so if that strengthens their position, because I heartily believe that if the Princess becomes Queen and declares herself in favour of these reforms, she will have the goodwill and fervent support of any true-born Englishman. And therefore I say plainly that if I plot against the King of England, it will be in the interest of the Stadhouder and his wife.'

'You do not deny, then, that you are plotting?'

'At this moment, I do deny it. I am simply reading a book and having my dinner. Do you see anyone with me? Does not a plot require accomplices?'

'It does,' I agreed. 'Mijnheer, I apologise for disturbing you. I trust we have both made our positions clear and that we understand each other. I will report to the Stadhouder accordingly.'

Locke seemed to relax. 'I should be grateful if you would, Master. And for my part, if I hear of any definite movement towards forwarding the Duke of Monmouth's interests, I shall be sure to communicate my knowledge to the Stadhouder. No doubt a letter to you at the University of Leiden would reach him discreetly.'

Don't bring me into this, I thought. *Write to him directly.*

But I said nothing.

CHAPTER ELEVEN

As we walked to meet the mayors, I relayed Locke's comments to Pringle.

'I think you have another report to write,' he said. 'But it can wait until you have a reply to your last one. I can't spare lots of men to go running back and forth to The Hague.'

Hudde came to meet me in the entrance hall. 'I fear, Master, that I was unable to persuade my fellow mayors,' he explained apologetically. 'They advanced an argument similar to your own, that it did not matter where our money went if it enabled the Stadhouder to fight his aggressive war.'

'That is a great shame,' I said.

'What will you do now?' he asked.

I had absolutely no idea, nor could I think of any way of giving the impression that I had.

'Our orders are to remain here until you acquiesce,' Pringle intervened, 'so that is what we must do. We apologise for the inconvenience. Of course, if our stay is to exceed a few days I must find more fitting accommodation for my men.'

Hudde blanched. No city likes having soldiers quartered on its citizens, even a small number of them. There is very little better designed to break down men's stubbornness than the thought that a number of lusty young soldiers with nothing to do except hang around taverns will be in town for the foreseeable future; and if they have daughters, the urgency to reach an agreement will be enhanced.

I am never quite sure why young women find soldiers attractive, since, in my experience, they tend to be insanitary and uncouth. The best that can be said for them is that they are away much of the time. However, Pringle's men were not going anywhere, as he had just explained.

'I am sure that we will continue to work towards a resolution,' Hudde mumbled unconvincingly.

'I hope so,' I agreed.

'Do you have any new proposals to put to us?' asked Hudde hopefully.

'None. I can only say what I have said before.'

There was a prolonged and awkward silence. There seemed to be no point in meeting the mayors if they had rejected my suggestion — which was actually Hudde's proposal in the first place — given that I had nothing more to offer.

'If you will excuse me, I must see to my men,' Pringle announced. What with Kees leaving me unattended and now Pringle vanishing, I began to feel deserted.

Hudde waited until Pringle had gone before speaking. 'Master, I wonder if you would consent to be our guest at a small musical entertainment this evening at Huydecoper's house? There will be a little supper and a consort of viols will play for us. I believe the programme is largely French, some works by Monsieur de Sainte-Colombe among others.'

'Thank you,' I replied, 'I should like that very much.'

I have never been good at lying. I give myself away, so I could only hope that my cheeks were not reddening as I told this blatant untruth. An evening of viol music was only slightly preferable to an evening of lute music, and the reader will know how I feel about lute players.

It is not that I am completely unappreciative of the musical art. There was a fiddle player in our village when I was a child who could hold me enraptured with his playing, and unlike many of my fellow Reformed ministers I could see a place for music in worship. It is just that sitting for a couple of hours trying to pay attention always makes me think of better things I could be doing with my time, like reading a good book; or polishing my boots, or learning to sew buttons on.

Anyway, I had committed myself now, and at least I could look forward to watching Huydecoper being compelled to be polite to me for an entire evening. If that didn't shorten the proceedings, I didn't know what would.

'Perhaps, in return, I could offer you the use of my carriage?' I found myself saying, though the term "my carriage" sounded very strange on my lips. I had assumed that Huydecoper would live hard by, and no carriage would be necessary, but it turned out that he lived on the Lauriergracht, about ten minutes' walk from Hudde's house, and the opportunity to keep mevrouw Hudde's gown out of the street filth was accepted with alacrity.

Having made the offer, I now had to find out how I summoned the carriage given that Kees and Pringle had both deserted me. I therefore excused myself to make the necessary arrangements, having engaged that the carriage would be outside the Huddes' door at a quarter of an hour before seven o'clock.

I found the warehouse where Pringle's men were quartered. He had just broken the news to them that they would be staying in Amsterdam a while longer. To my surprise, instead of consternation the news appeared to be received with equanimity. As I entered several of the soldiers were discussing the charms of young ladies whom they had met in Amsterdam, and whom they hoped to see again. It appeared that several of these women shared an address, and it took me a few minutes to realise what class of women the men were talking about.

I suppose I should be more censorious about such irregular connections, but I have seen enough of the world to realise that many such women have turned to vice in desperation, not because of a want of morals. This makes their fall doubly tragic; imagine having to adopt a trade of which you deeply disapprove. It is almost unthinkable. My views on the matter had been largely transformed by the comments of Fat Lysbeth, who plied her trade outside the gates of the university but who was often to be found in Steen's inn, particularly when the weather was bitter. She was very open about her business, but considered that she had one great advantage over a wife, namely that she could refuse her favours if she so chose. After all, she said, married women please their men in return for comfort and security, and so did she.

'But surely,' I said on one occasion, 'they are motivated by love for their husbands?'

'Love?' Fat Lysbeth replied. 'How many women find love in marriage? I'll tell you, mijnheer, that poor women may marry for love, for there's no other advantage to them in it, but these wretched girls who live their lives in silk are just chattels. Their husbands are more likely to love their horses than their wives.'

I had come to understand her argument with the passage of the years. There were exceptions, of course. Johannes Voet and his wife were devoted to each other; Hudde treated his wife with genuine affection. My brief stay with Johannes's grandfather in Utrecht had shown me an old couple who had enjoyed each other's company for many years; and although the Stadhouder had married Princess Mary for reasons of state, yet he had come to admire her good sense and utter loyalty to him and would be much grieved when she died young — but I get ahead of my story.

Pringle was very pleased when I outlined my plans for the evening. 'Excellent. We must ensure that you are seen to arrive with some display.'

'I'd really rather not,' I protested.

'As Master Mercurius, you may make that choice,' Pringle answered, 'but as the representative of the Stadhouder, you must exemplify his power. No, I shall ensure that you make an impression on Huydecoper's guests.'

He then addressed his men. Since he did so in English and my grasp of that language is not perfect, I am unable to record his remarks exactly, but he used several terms that I might have considered abusive, questioning the parentage of many of them and insisting that their uniforms must be pristine that evening, though, of course, a cabbage wrapped in gold leaf is still a cabbage. They appeared not to take offence, but one shouted that they might be pond scum but they were proud to be Pringle's scum. They set to polishing their kit to the accompaniment of a song about a young lady from somewhere called Paddington who was, it seemed, a great friend to soldiers. I just hoped that they would not sing it outside the musical soirée that evening, especially the verse about what she would do for twopence if she liked you.

The arrangements having been made, I decided to return to seek out mijnheer Pereyra. I felt my work with the English was done, that there was nothing I could do to further the matter of Amsterdam's taxes, but at least I could keep my promise to investigate the disappearance of the children.

Pereyra greeted me pleasantly, which made me feel all the more uncomfortable about what I had to say.

'The more I learn, mijnheer, the more I feel that the kidnapper is someone who knows your community well. In short, he may be one of you,' I said.

Pereyra did not shout or challenge me to a duel, but I could see he was unhappy. 'I am not blind to appearances,' he replied. 'But we have searched the area. Little Isidore has been gone six months. I cannot conceive of any way in which he could be among us without being noticed.' He sighed. 'Master, we are a close-knit people. Adversity has forced that upon us. I do not claim that we are especially virtuous, but there are some sins that are less likely among us because we share that history. When one of us weeps, we all weep. We travelled from Spain to Portugal together. Now we have come here together, in search of a place of peace where we can raise our children in safety. We cannot express how grateful we are to your people for allowing us to settle here. We keep our own ways, but we try to be good Dutchmen too. A man who jeopardises this for us is an animal and should be slaughtered as one.'

There was no doubting the sincerity of Pereyra's words. His eyes glistened with tears as he spoke.

'Every one of us has allowed his house to be searched. All the men joined in a search of barges at the quays after each disappearance. Of course, we are not the only inhabitants of these streets, though many of our Christian neighbours have joined us in our searches. But I am as confident as I can be that none of us was responsible for this villainy.' He sat heavily on a stool. 'Nevertheless, I accept that my conviction is not evidence for you. Master, you may go anywhere you like. Perhaps your eyes will see something to which we have been blind. Tomorrow is Friday. If you come to the synagogue just before sunset, the Rabbi will commend you to our whole people and instruct them to give you every assistance.'

'I will gladly do so. And I am sorry to sow suspicion like this. But I must exhaust every line of enquiry.'

'Of course.'

'Forgive my ignorance, but surely the synagogue will be filled with your people. That does not include those other Jews who have their own synagogue.'

'The Ashkenazim?'

'If that is what you call those Jews who are not Portuguese.'

'The majority of the Ashkenazim here have arrived from Germany and the Baltic coast. They speak a different language to us, though we can converse in Hebrew, up to a point. We do not bear each other any great animosity, but we have lived different lives. We have different histories. We are people of the sun; they have been in Northern Europe for centuries. We live comfortable lives; they are poor, for the most part. Of course, simple charity requires us to have some care for them.'

'Could an Ashkenazi Jew be responsible for this?'

Pereyra was appalled. 'I pray you, do not say so aloud! It is no small thing you say. If my people believed that one of them was responsible, I do not know what evil would result. Unless we have clear evidence, we must not raise the subject publicly, or I cannot vouch for the safety of any man.' He ran his hands through his thick black hair and sat awhile staring at his feet. 'Master, you must understand that for as long as my people can recall, nobody has defended us. We have had to be self-reliant. Now we have come here, and we have found a welcome. But in adversity there are those among us who believe that we must look after our own interests with torches and cudgels and all the nasty apparatus of mob rule. I have argued that we are among a civilised people who will protect our interests if we are patient. When you appeared among us I rejoiced. At last we were blessed with an official who would take our complaints seriously and right the wrongs we had suffered. I still believe that offers us our best chance; but I cannot discount the fear that some men are waiting for an opportunity to take their revenge on anyone they can blame. If peace is to be maintained, we have to find an answer to this riddle, and we must find it together.'

I stood for a moment in thought. There was much truth in Pereyra's words; and just as he feared that some Jews would take matters into their own hands if the authorities were not seen to act, so I knew that there would be Christians only too happy to resort to the sword and the flame in retaliation. Amsterdam could erupt in unfettered destruction, and with so many Jews among us they would not be a persecuted minority who could be subdued in an afternoon. This would be a much more even contest.

In view of this calculation, I was surprised that the mayors were not taking the matter more seriously. These were not stupid men; well, no more stupid than mayors everywhere. They had, perhaps, lost sight of what mattered most about their role, ensuring the peaceful and secure life of their citizens. They had become enmeshed in business, in mistaking private prosperity for the chief goal of the mayoralty, but I could not understand how they could not see this. Or maybe they could, but just did not care because these were the children of immigrants.

I remembered a little village I had once visited in the tip of Flanders. Within the knowledge of the oldest inhabitant, it had been part of France, of the Spanish Netherlands, maybe even of some German state. Armies went back and forth, sowing destruction behind them, and the ordinary people woke up to find they were now part of some other land. A new flag flew, and a set of marker posts set out a new boundary, but their lives went on. The cattle continued to give milk and meat, and I do not suppose that they thought of themselves as belonging to a particular nation.

Are we any happier for having created states? Are we confined by imaginary lines that men have drawn on maps? Isidore, Shmuel and Daniel had all been born here. They were as Dutch as I was. What made them "immigrants" when they have never lived anywhere else? For myself, I was proud that outsiders found our lands so attractive that they yearned to live here, and that the Stadhouder did not seek to exclude them.

I could not express these thoughts to mijnheer Pereyra. I simply sat on a stool beside him, and we discussed what I had seen on my last visit to the district, hoping that by turning it over once again something — anything! — might jump out and open the matter to us.

But it was in vain.

The carriage had been washed until it gleamed. Lanterns were fixed to each corner and the coachmen were immaculate. Pringle and his troops were lined up to escort us and even Kees looked less of a mess than usual, having been persuaded to brush his coat. I wondered how he would arrive at the Lauriergracht with us, since the cart was not being used this evening, but it seemed that once the Huddes were inside the carriage Kees would be permitted to cling to the back, so long as he kept out of sight.

I invited my guests to climb inside and took my seat opposite them.

'This is extremely kind of you, Master,' Hudde said. It was good to see him smile. He, at least, was looking forward to his evening.

It was a short trip to Huydecoper's town house. We could probably have walked it quicker, because we were held up by the need to marshal the horses and clear a path along the streets large enough to allow us to pass, but in around a quarter of an hour we were there. I felt, rather than saw, Kees leap from the back. Not having had a manservant before, I was unsure what he was doing there, but Pringle assured me it was all part of the display. He would, I learned, be sitting in the kitchen waiting for any instruction that I might have, and possibly lending a hand to Huydecoper's own servants.

I assisted Hudde's wife from the carriage, and we stepped inside. Huydecoper was, of course, a rich man. He had his country home at Maarsseveen but his town house would have sufficed for many. Rather than living in the fashionable streets where the other mayors lived, he had chosen to make a home in an area much favoured by artists and musicians. He took great delight in taking me to a window and pointing out the homes of various neighbours, several of whom I had never heard of but did not like to say so, since everyone else was raising their eyebrows appreciatively to acknowledge that we were surrounded by such men.

We were shown to our seats, and the music began. I was, it seems, regarded as the guest of honour and was therefore in the middle of the front row. This was unfortunate because it meant that I was unable to nod off during the performance as usual. This is not rampant philistinism on my part; there is some strange chemistry that means that as soon as a consort of music starts up, my eyelids begin to feel heavy and my head commences a gentle nodding. As luck would have it, Huydecoper's wife Sophia was sitting beside me, and she had dressed herself with some perfume that effectively prevented somnolence, since I required all my concentration to keep breathing. I do not know what it was but it was as subtle as an ox dancing a pavane.

After about an hour we were invited to refresh ourselves with wines and cordials. I mistakenly believed that this signalled the end of the concert, but in short order we were invited to return to our seats for a second period of misery before a rousing finale indicated that the programme was concluded.

I had, of course, reckoned without the audience's demand for an encore. I can understand that when people have paid for their tickets and want to extract the maximum for their money, but when admission is free it smacks to me of self-indulgence.

The consort duly took up their viols one more time, and I was relieved when that was greeted with polite applause and no further demands for new pieces.

We were invited to partake of the "little supper". Dear reader, I have seen banquets that were on a smaller scale. New platters appeared with regularity. I even noticed Kees helping with one, a particularly delicate sugar confection that had to be manoeuvred round a corner and set on a table; on which, of course, someone had just placed a goblet in the only suitable space.

At length we had all eaten as much as we could, though the table still looked very full to me, and we thanked our host and hostess and waddled to our carriage. I noticed that Kees was not with us, and wondered what the correct etiquette was for retrieving an errant servant, but in the nick of time a side door opened and Kees appeared, apparently detained by some female hand which refused to let him go. He gently prised himself free and blew a kiss into the darkness before racing to clamber on the back of the carriage.

I was going to have to have a word with that boy.

CHAPTER TWELVE

Having been deprived of any sleep during the concert, I was quite tired when we reached Hudde's house and would gladly have ascended the stairs to my chamber at once, but one of Pringle's men was loitering in the hallway with a letter in his hand. As if the evening had not been bad enough, I saw at once that it bore the Stadhouder's seal. Not only that, he had addressed it himself. There was no mistaking his handwriting.

I thanked him and ripped it open.

You have done well. I did not expect a resolution with Amsterdam, so I am not surprised that you have not achieved it. I am now moving towards Apeldoorn with an army and, in due time, we will come to Amsterdam to sort things out. At least your efforts have shown that I tried to conclude the matter amicably. While you're there you might want to look for some suitable place where a hanged man would have the greatest impact on the locals.

You had to admire William's sense of practicality.

As for the matter of the Portuguese children, I am delighted that you have taken this up. No doubt you will bring the matter to a successful conclusion, thus demonstrating to all the abject inadequacy of the Amsterdam authorities.

That was not what I needed to hear at that moment. Something more along the lines of "If you fail, it does not matter" would have been much more welcome.

If you need to write to me again, Mercurius, I'll be at Utrecht for a few days. It's nearer to Amsterdam than Apeldoorn in case I need to divert my army.

I took it that William had no real intention of going to Apeldoorn and that this was just a subterfuge to disguise his plan to ride through Amsterdam with an army and put the fear of the Almighty into the inhabitants so that they would hand over their taxes with no further demur.

'Bad news, Master?' asked Hudde.

It is for you, I thought. 'The Stadhouder is anxious that we should conclude matters speedily,' I replied. The letter did not say that, but I think I could justifiably claim that it was implied. 'To that end, he is moving nearer to Amsterdam to be available should his assistance be required.'

'How close?' Hudde asked nervously.

'To Utrecht for the moment.'

I am sure that Hudde shuddered. He knew as well as I did what this intelligence portended. We stood in awkward silence for a minute or so before Hudde suggested that we repair to a more private place and ushered me into his study.

'Can we agree, Master, that what is said in this place goes no further and is between the two of us?'

'Willingly,' I answered.

'I fear that the arrival of the Stadhouder in our city, welcome though he will always be, will be counter-productive.'

'How so?'

'It will harden attitudes. Even if he wins this battle, hostilities will break out again as soon as he leaves. His every move will be opposed simply because it is his move. We must redouble our efforts to settle the matter before he comes.'

'I agree, mijnheer,' I replied, 'but I have no idea how.'

'Neither have I,' Hudde answered. 'But we have to think of something.'

I mulled over William's letter once more. It occurred to me that it could be read in a particular way; that my task of convincing the mayors had failed, but was now over, and that all my efforts should now be directed towards discovering the fate of the Portuguese children. Since that suited me very well, and Hudde had not actually seen the letter to form his own opinion, I decided to construe it in that light.

'I am commanded by the Stadhouder now to bend all my efforts towards discovering the fate of the Portuguese children,' I announced.

Hudde was taken aback. 'So there will be no further discussions?'

'It appears not. If there are any, the Stadhouder will conduct them himself.'

Hudde's consternation was clear. 'Of course, we will do all in our power to assist with your enquiries,' he stammered, 'but I entreat you to do all in your power to keep our dialogue going. Frankly, I have more hope of success in a dialogue with you than with the Stadhouder.'

'It is not my place to disobey the Stadhouder's instructions,' I answered, 'and frankly you have observed yourself that we have no progress to report. It isn't as if I could assure him that agreement is near and he need not be so hasty.'

'Of course, of course...' murmured Hudde. 'I wasn't suggesting...' His voice tailed away as if he did not know exactly what he was suggesting. 'If you will excuse me, I must hurriedly confer with my colleagues,' he said.

I saw a small opportunity, like a little candle briefly flickering in the darkness. 'I suppose,' I mused, 'that given the lateness of the hour, I might not have opened this letter until tomorrow morning. In which event, of course, I would not know that I am to break off discussions just yet.'

Hudde's face lit up. 'Yes, I see that!' he exclaimed. 'Thank you for your understanding, Master.'

He ran from the room to send messages to his fellow mayors while I retired to my chamber to think things through. Kees was occupied in laying out a clean shirt when I entered but looked up with a broad smile on his face.

'Did you enjoy your evening, Master?' he asked.

'I've had bet— never mind *my* evening! What of *your* evening, you blackguard?'

'Master?'

'Don't play the innocent with me, Kees. I saw you with that maid. I did not take you to the Huydecopers' house for you to ravage their servants!'

'If I may be bold, Master, you didn't take me at all. You had no need of me there, you told Captain Pringle.'

'Yes! Quite right! He was the one who insisted you come with me. It would impress them to see that I had a manservant, he said.'

Kees did not answer.

'But instead of comporting yourself like a gentleman's manservant, you passed your evening carousing in the kitchen and seducing a young girl.'

'She wasn't that young,' he protested.

'Her age is not the point! She is under Huydecoper's roof and her conduct is a matter for his oversight. He is entitled to feel that my manservant groping his maids is a serious breach of etiquette.'

'Master, you're becoming overheated.'

I have a temper. There is no point in denying the fact. It does not surface often, but when it does I am apt to forget myself. While I was annoyed at Kees's coolness, I could not deny that matters were, perhaps, becoming a little heated.

'Maybe it would help, Master, if I told you a little more of my activities tonight.'

'I do not want to hear the lurid details of your sexual conquests.'

'There were none, Master — and if there were, I would keep them to myself. The Captain asked me to undertake a little job for him because I could gain entry to the house and he could not.'

Now I was intrigued. 'A little job for him? Let him use his own servants. You're supposed to be mine, aren't you?'

'I am, Master. But it may help if we keep our voices down while I apologise for a small necessary deception.'

'Deception? You have deceived me too?'

'I have, Master, and I am sorry for it, and I should still be doing so but I fear that if I do not explain now our relationship will be damaged beyond repair.'

'Relationship? We don't have a relationship. So far as I can see, you do what you want and occasionally show up when you need feeding.'

Kees lowered his eyes and took a deep breath. 'My name, Master, is Kees. That much is true. But I am Lieutenant Kees van Vliet. I was sent here to masquerade as your servant while seeking out information that may be of advantage to the Stadhouder.'

I was flabbergasted. I was so shocked that I sat down heavily. It would have helped if there had been a chair behind me. Trying to rise from the floor with some sense of dignity, I grasped his arm to pull myself up, so that our faces came close together. 'I had no idea. How could I be so wrong about a person?'

'Don't reproach yourself, Master. I take it as a tribute to my acting. It is true that I have been very friendly to the maids, but I give you my word that there has been no impropriety.'

'No impropriety? Your entire mission is an impropriety. I have brought a wolf in sheep's clothing into my host's house!'

'I mean that the girls are as pure now as they were before I came.'

'Girls? Plural? I should have you gelded before you cause any more mischief.'

'It is necessary that I should make myself amiable to them so that they will share the knowledge that they have,' Kees explained.

'What knowledge can maids possibly have that is of use to the Stadhouder?'

'You would be surprised, Master. In fact, you will be surprised when I tell you. But I must ask you to control your voice. We must not be discovered.'

'We? Don't you dare bring me into this! I am a minister of the Church. I can't be seen to be turning a blind eye to this debauchery.'

'Nobody has been debauched, Master. We just had a little fun.'

'And in nine months' time will it seem such fun to her?'

'We didn't get to that. We didn't have time during the concert.'

'Thank goodness for that. If the performance had been an opera, who knows what villainy might have been committed during the evening?'

'Master, pray calm yourself. You will suffer an apoplexy.' I mopped my face with a kerchief. I suppose I must have been very red, for my cheeks were burning. 'The thing is, Master, that I was after Huydecoper's book.'

'A book? In the maid's bedroom?'

'No, Master. In his bedroom.'

'He has a library full of books downstairs, Kees. You might have had more luck finding a book there.'

'This is not a book he reads, Master. This is a book he writes.'

'You speak in riddles, Kees.'

'You will have noticed, Master, how others defer to Huydecoper although he is not the senior mayor. In fact, others do his will without argument. Why is it, do you suppose?'

'Maybe it's because he is a nice person.'

'You've met him, Master. Do you think he is a nice person?'

'Well, I … my views don't come into this. Explain yourself.'

'It has been common gossip for some time that mijnheer Huydecoper keeps a book in which he records all the gifts he gives and receives.'

This struck me as quite a good idea. It must be embarrassing if someone comes to visit and you forget the little present they gave you last time.

'By gifts, Master, I do not mean trinkets. He keeps accounts of all the bribes he gives and accepts, to whom they were made and for what purpose, and what recompense was received from them in exchange for those favours.'

I flopped down again. At least this time I landed on the bed. 'A book full of bribes?'

'So it was said, Master. Some merchants in Amsterdam were surprised that he could recall details of all their previous transactions and suggested that he might be in league with the Devil, but a former servant of his is understood to have let it be known that such a book exists.'

I rubbed my chin in thought. It might explain his motives. There may be people to whom he was beholden who had some grip over him. Or, in the alternative, he might be able to expect favours from others to forward schemes to his own advantage. 'I'd love to know what is in that book,' I whispered.

'Wonder no more,' said Kees with a smile, as he lifted my pillow to reveal a book bound in black leather.

I may have shrieked. In any event, I found myself exceedingly agitated. 'You've brought it into my room?'

'Well, Master, I can hardly keep it in the kitchen, can I? And remember that I sleep here too.'

'When you're not sleeping with that dark-haired maid.'

'There's no harm in sleeping with a maid,' he grinned. 'It's when you stay awake that the mischief is done.'

'Tell me no more!'

'Anyway, Master, I wasn't getting much sleep what with your snoring.'

'I do not snore,' I replied indignantly.

'Have it your way, Master, but somebody in the room was snoring and it wasn't me, for I couldn't sleep.'

My eyes were drawn back again to that black thing under my pillow. 'What are you planning we should do with that?' I demanded.

'Use the information within it to our advantage, of course.'

'What information?'

'I don't know. I don't know most of the people mentioned.'

'Neither will I. I know nobody in Amsterdam.'

'But with respect, Master, that doesn't matter. All that matters is that Huydecoper should realise that his book is missing, and that you've seen it. You'll have a hold over him because he will know his transactions may soon be exposed to the light of day.'

'Yes, Kees, and he may decide the best way to stop that happening is to have my throat slit.'

Kees shrugged. 'That's why I'm here.'

'To slit my throat? You might as well do so, since you've set me up for it.'

'No, Master, to stop others doing it.'

'Until you got to work, Kees, nobody wanted my throat cut.'

'You'd be surprised, Master. I've heard it mentioned two or three times. Not by mijnheer Hudde, I'm pleased to say, but the other gentlemen don't seem to be too fond of you.'

'And now one of them has every reason to act upon his wish.'

'Master, you're becoming overwrought.'

'Do you wonder at that? It's a fault of mine. I overreact when people talk about killing me. Believe me, Kees, I've had someone come at me with a knife to silence me. It's not pleasant.'

'Life at the university must be wilder than I thought,' Kees commented.

'It wasn't at the university. It was in an alley … oh, never mind. Take the book away and burn it. Throw it away. Chuck it in a canal.'

'None of those will work, Master. When Huydecoper finds his book is missing, he'll assume you have it even if you don't.'

There was some truth in this. He would think it suspicious that his book would disappear on the very evening when I was in his house.

'Where was the book?' I asked.

Kees smiled ruefully. 'It took some finding. It was in a drawer in his bedroom under his shirts.'

'Did you search the whole house?'

'No, Trijntje told me it was in his bedroom.'

'Why would she tell you that?'

'She is out of countenance with him over the matter of a holiday to visit her mother that he cancelled. And I gave her half a guilder.'

'Half a guilder?'

'Don't worry, I'll claim it back on my expenses. You won't have to pay it.'

'I should think not!'

'It's a big room and it took me quite a while to get the information out of her. Then when I helped to bring in the sugar confection, I didn't go back to the kitchen. She would think I was required in the main room, since the maids were all kept below stairs. But I hadn't managed to find it when I heard the consort finishing their performance, so I had to improvise.'

'In what way?'

'I sneaked into the room at the back and called for an encore. Fortunately, others took up the cry and during those extra minutes I was able to uncover it.'

My head was spinning. Not only had I had to endure additional viol playing, but my own servant had caused it. I had not been so incapable of understanding what I was hearing since I'd listened to one of the undergraduates attempt to precis my series of lectures on Thomas à Kempis, whom he seemed to think was two people, Thomas and Kempis.

'I think, Kees, that we should go to bed now, and perhaps when I wake up in the morning I'll discover this was all just a bad dream, and I haven't been made an involuntary receiver of property stolen from a man whose hospitality I was enjoying at the time.'

'Surely you didn't enjoy that?' Kees asked.

I nearly threw the book at him.

CHAPTER THIRTEEN

Despite my reservations about its provenance, in the morning I read Huydecoper's book. Do not judge me. Reading books is what I do.

It was exactly as boring as I feared it might be. After all, it was just a catalogue of presents given and received. I had hoped that there might be an entry along the lines of "Gave 1000 guilders to X to foment an uprising against the Stadhouder" but there was not; instead there were great lists of women who had given birth to babies (none of them Huydecoper's), men who were getting married, people who had given him information to help him make money, and so on.

In a few places he had annotated an earlier entry to note, for example, that someone had not performed the promised service and therefore should expect no more gifts, or that he had overpaid for the service provided. There was a smaller number of instances where someone had treated him generously and Huydecoper had reminded himself to make some recompense when the opportunity arose.

The astute reader might wonder why Huydecoper had not written the book in some code or cipher, as I did myself. I think the answer is that he needed to be able to find the information he needed quickly, and there were simply too many people mentioned for a code to be practical. There were abbreviations, but I do not think those would have long detained anyone who knew a few people in Amsterdam. It did not take much, for example, to divine that "HV" stood for

Heer Van. What was noticeable was the lack of any gifts for the Stadhouder, at least on any of the pages that I read.

All in all, I think it was the second most boring book I had ever read; and, no, I am not going to give the title of the most boring one. I do not wish to offend a fellow lecturer.

When I descended to breakfast, I was informed that Hudde had left early to attend an urgent meeting of his fellow mayors. He respectfully suggested that it might be "convenient" if I were to amuse myself until, say, eleven o'clock when I might amble over to see what conclusions the mayors had reached. This suited me very well, because it gave me some time to brief Pringle on the extraordinary events of the previous evening.

I guessed that he might be with his men, and so it proved, though at the moment of my arrival he was inspecting the state of the horses, so I left him undisturbed. Some of the Englishmen were playing a game at cards and, thinking it might be an intellectual challenge to my brain, I decided to see if I could deduce how the game was played.

I failed dismally. So far as I could tell, each player looked at his own cards and tried to judge whether they were a better or worse set than those of the other players. If they were worse, he threw them down on the board and played no part. If, however, he judged that his were superior, he wagered a sum. The next person had then to decide whether to wager the same sum or a greater one. Eventually, the game ended in one of two ways; either the players agreed to display their hands, in which event the better combination of cards took the winnings, or all the players threw their cards down and the last man to do so was the winner; but — and here was the part that puzzled me — he threw his cards face down too.

'Shouldn't he prove that he had the best hand?' I asked.

'Bless you, dominie, where's the sport in that?' one replied. 'We'll never know whether he actually had three matching cards or not, but he bet as if he did.'

'Forgive my obtuseness,' I said, 'but doesn't that reward deceit and untruthfulness? Surely the biggest bluffer will win every time.'

'Ah, no, Master,' another explained. 'You see, we know each other. And the longer we play together, the better we know each other. George here will only bet on a good hand, so as soon as he pushes his coins forward we all throw ours in, and he wins next to nothing. When Matthew has a good hand, his eyes light up.' He pointed to a soldier who was cleaning his gun. 'Solomon doesn't play with us often because when he's about to tell a lie, his lip twitches and we all know; isn't that right, Solomon?'

The soldier growled some sort of response, which I suspect may have been an English expression of a low character.

'But the best players, like Jack here, can keep a straight face whatever cards they have, which makes them difficult to play against. I've stood behind Jack when he was playing and seen him stake a huge sum on a completely useless hand, but because he displayed such confidence all the other players folded their cards and let him win. It's all about who can bluff successfully when they need to.'

'What an unholy entertainment this must be if it requires men to lie to be successful!' I remarked.

'No, Master, begging your pardon. Jack doesn't lie. He allows people to come to the wrong conclusion, that's all. It's not his fault if they guess wrong, is it? He hasn't deceived them. He has only used his money as he thinks fit. If they make assumptions based on his play that are wrong, how is that Jack's fault?'

I cannot say that I was entirely convinced, but clearly I needed to give some longer consideration to the ethics of card-playing when I had some leisure. I thanked them for their explanation and wandered over to see Pringle, who had completed his inspection. 'It seems that I have been deceived as to the nature of Kees's service,' I said.

'I know,' Pringle replied.

'Why wasn't I told that he was not what he appeared to be?' I asked.

Pringle seemed surprised by the question. 'Why, because you are an honest man. I doubt you could have kept the secret. Even now, I'm debating whether I need to withdraw Kees before you give the game away.'

'He may need withdrawing before he pledges himself to half the young women of Amsterdam!' I remarked with some passion.

'Yes,' smiled Pringle, 'he has some talent in that direction, doesn't he? I wonder what his knack is?'

'Whatever it is, it is not to be admired or emulated,' I snapped. 'Nor is his ability to spirit away other people's possessions. He stole a book from Huydecoper's house last night.'

'I know,' said Pringle.

'You know?'

'Yes. I asked him to do so. Or, more accurately, I told him of the rumours that such a book existed and asked him to see if he could verify them. I didn't expect that he would succeed so well as actually to lay hands on the book. I thought it would be locked away somewhere.'

I looked about me for prying eyes. Seeing none, I reached inside my cloak and slipped the book to him. 'Here it is.'

To my alarm, he opened it publicly and began to leaf through its pages.

'What are you doing?' I hissed.

'Looking for dirt on Huydecoper. What else would I be doing?'

'This is an invasion of privacy,' I protested.

Pringle frowned. 'I suppose you're right,' he said. 'But then how would we ever uncover conspiracies, because surely by definition every conspiracy is private?'

I was flustered by this question. 'That's completely different,' I expostulated.

'In what way is it different? Enlighten us, Master.'

'I would have to give that some mature consideration,' I answered.

'While you're doing so, perhaps I can suggest a factor which might bear upon your thinking, Master. The sooner we get the mayors to agree to hand over their taxes, the sooner you can get back to your books, and if using this book of Huydecoper's helps us to achieve that, isn't that a good thing?'

'Ethics are not to be determined by my personal advantage,' I said. I will admit it sounded rather pompous, even as I was saying it.

'Shall I tell Kees to take it back, then?' Pringle demanded.

'Let us not be rash,' I replied. 'There may be a greater good involved here.'

'Exactly what I was thinking,' said Pringle.

'Since you knew of this book and I didn't, is there anything else it may be advantageous to me to know?'

'I don't know, Master. I don't know what you don't know.'

We strolled to the City Hall to resume discussions. There was no point in haste. Indeed, being dilatory might encourage them to get to the point.

As we entered, a couple of servants were waiting for us. One approached me with a letter. You can imagine my feelings when I saw that it was from the Stadhouder.

I carefully opened it and read the contents. It told me nothing that I did not already know. In many respects, it mirrored the second half of his letter I had received on the previous evening.

Suddenly, it dawned on me that this letter was not really for me. It was intended for the mayors. This was clear from the fact that William had endorsed it above the seal with the date and the word "Utrecht". He just wanted the mayors to know he was coming for them.

I showed the letter to Pringle.

'Excellent!' he said.

We continued to mount the stairs, but Pringle pulled at my arm to hold me back.

'Master, there is something I don't know that may mean something to you.'

'Indeed?'

'As the mayors were arriving for their discussion this morning, one of my men heard Van Beuningen say that he hoped we would not find out about "the Panama adventure".'

'How did your men hear that? Weren't they all in their quarters?'

'It depends how you define "my men", Master. I may have augmented them since our arrival.'

'You mean that you have bribed someone?'

'Bribed is an ugly word. I prefer to say that we have recruited one or two of the City Hall servants.'

'One or two? Is it one, or two?'

'Three, if you're being pedantic.'

'I'm being accurate.'

'Be that as it may,' Pringle continued, 'there is plainly something they don't want us to know about, and therefore that's the very thing we must bend our efforts towards uncovering.'

We were admitted to the large chamber where we seemed to be interrupting a heated argument. Huydecoper stopped speaking in mid-sentence and greetings were exchanged before we were invited to sit.

'Is there any point?' I asked. 'You may know that there was a letter waiting for me here. I have it in my hand. You are welcome to read it.'

I gave it to Geelvinck, who was nearest to me. He glanced over it, then passed it to Van Beuningen, who was visibly agitated by what he read; so much so that he sat with the letter in his hand and Huydecoper had to wrest it from him.

'You will see,' I explained, 'that the Stadhouder's patience is almost exhausted. In the circumstances I am not sure that there is anything to be gained in continuing our discussions.'

Hudde was quick to intervene. 'Let us pause a moment,' he suggested. 'We are in danger of causing a serious rift that will take some healing.'

Huydecoper was unconcerned. 'We have reached an impasse. The Master has his instructions, and we are charged with defending our city's interests. They do not coincide. There is no point in trying to gloss over this disagreement.'

'I agree,' I said. 'I will now retire to attend to my other duties.'

'Other duties?' asked Geelvinck.

'I am instructed by the Stadhouder to investigate the disappearance of the Portuguese children and whether any local officials have been derelict in their duty.' I could have sworn that Van Beuningen whimpered.

I took a few paces towards the door. 'I do not know when the Stadhouder will come,' I announced, 'but if you have anything to say before that day, I shall be happy to attend upon you. You will find me in the Jewish quarter.'

As we descended to the street Pringle seemed very pleased.

'Well handled, Master. That has given them food for thought.'

'I'd love to know what is being said in that room now,' I answered him.

'You will, Master, you will,' he assured me.

One of the results of all the activity over the past few days had been that I had not been able to find any time to myself to think. If I'd felt inadequate to the tasks set for me before, that feeling was intensified by recent events. I did not feel that I was making any headway with the missing Portuguese children, the negotiations for the Stadhouder's taxes had gone nowhere, and if I had reached an understanding of sorts with mijnheer Locke, we now had the mysterious reference to Panama to investigate. I began to ponder whether I could just go back to Leiden and wait there. If I decamped to Steen's inn, they might not find me there; although, if they had any brains and did not find me in my room, that was the obvious place to search next.

Accordingly, I suggested to Pringle that he should leave me alone for a little while and I would find somewhere to turn matters over in my brain. I did not go far in my search for a tavern where I might sit and think.

One of the great things about taverns is that wherever in the world you are, a tavern is not hard to find. Their owners take considerable pains to ensure that thirsty people can spot their premises, and thus I had no difficulty in picking out the establishment that received my custom.

It looked a higher class of place than some in Amsterdam. There were no sailors or whores for a start — or, more accurately, nobody immediately identifiable as a whore — and a number of customers whose dress marked them as gentlemen.

I sat at a table and stared into space until my ale was brought. At an adjoining table, a man was engrossed in reading some sort of news-sheet and making marks in a ledger. He caught me inspecting him and nodded a greeting.

'Forgive me,' I said. 'I didn't mean to stare.'

The man smiled pleasantly. 'That's all right. I didn't think what I was doing was so interesting. I assume that you are not a trader.'

'A trader?'

'In commodities, stocks, shares, bonds, that kind of thing.'

It was my turn to smile. 'No, I'm a lecturer at the University of Leiden.'

'The badge on your collar suggests that you may be more than that.'

I glanced downwards. 'Oh, that. I'm here on some official business.'

He raised his tankard. 'Let us hope it is successful.'

I followed suit. 'I wish you well in yours.'

'I can't complain. No ships have been lost lately, and our overseas trade is very healthy.'

His remark brought something to mind. 'Maybe you can enlighten me. I have heard mention of some business in Panama. Do you know anything of it?'

'I know something. It is a project promoted by a young Scottish gentleman lately arrived here, mijnheer Paterson.'

'A Scot?'

'Yes, but he has lived for some time in the Caribbean. The plan he proposes is very simple. It depends upon the knowledge that Panama is a very narrow country. You will know, I am sure, that our trade with the Far East is extensive and valuable. We bring porcelain from China, silks from India and China, and spices and exotic wood from the East Indies. The voyage is long and difficult, and it entails some danger. The most difficult part is rounding the tip of Africa or South America, where there are fierce storms. Paterson's notion is that it would be much quicker to sail to the west coast of Panama, transport the cargo across the narrow neck of land to another ship on the east coast, and sail home from there.'

'If it is so simple, why has it not been done before?'

'The transport across the country is not straightforward. But Paterson has identified a large inlet on the west coast that would shorten the journey considerably. It would be no more than sixty miles or so. However, it is thick jungle. He aims to carve a road through and came here in search of canal engineers who could use his road to create a canal large enough for the ships to sail directly through without the need to unload.'

'A bold scheme indeed!' I remarked.

'Yes, it is. He is seeking investors, but he needs a large amount of capital. There are not many men with the money and the nerve necessary to invest in this.'

I decided to chance my arm. 'I have heard that mijnheer Van Beuningen has interested himself in the business.'

The man chuckled. 'Yes, he is very enthusiastic. May I ask, is he a friend of yours?'

'Say, rather, that we have recently become acquainted.'

'Then I hope you will not mind my saying that mijnheer Van Beuningen is not an investor whom more sober men might wish to emulate.'

'Do you think the project will not succeed?'

My informant took a draught of his beer and turned my question over in his mind. 'It promises huge rewards, but it is very risky. Consider a few facts. It is true that we have dug canals of that length in our country, but we have never tried to do so in a tropical jungle. Nor is clearing jungle from a road straightforward; it grows back and needs to be cleared again. But these are not the major concerns.'

'No?' I asked. They seemed fairly major to me.

'No. Paterson is assuming that the water is at the same level at each end of his putative canal, but because the tides are not synchronised that will not be so. And, more importantly, Panama is part of the Spanish Empire. It is hard to imagine that the Spaniards will leave us in quiet possession of it if we do not have their agreement in the first place. If we do not, then we must garrison it, and given that Spain is above a thousand miles nearer than we are to Panama, we will need a fast fleet to deliver reinforcements there if Spain moves to take it.'

My informant made a good case against the project, which led to another question. 'I am grateful to you for that analysis, mijnheer,' I said, 'which leads me to wonder why some men are so strongly for it?'

My neighbour tossed some coins on the table to pay for his drinks. 'There's your answer. They can see the profit if it succeeds. And they hope to persuade the Stadhouder to send the Dutch fleet to defend the seaways to Panama.'

So that was why the mayors were so keen to avoid war with France. They wanted the navy for their own use. This was obviously vital information. The question remained, though: how best to use it?

CHAPTER FOURTEEN

My first idea was to go straight to the City Hall and confront the miscreants, for that is what they were. They were pursuing their personal ambitions under cover of their office. It is, I suppose, possible that they had convinced themselves that their interests and Amsterdam's coincided. I do not impugn their sincerity; but think of the incident in the eighth chapter of the Gospel according to St Mark, where Jesus tells his disciples what is to befall him, and Peter tells him that the crucifixion need not happen, and is rebuked in his turn. By which we see that it is possible for a man to be sincere yet very wrong.

What was to be gained by facing them, I wondered? When it came to politics, I was as an infant. It had never interested me, and I knew nothing of it. Whatever I said, they would continue to be mayors, and even if I appealed to the electors of Amsterdam, these were men of exactly the same stamp. Who knew but that they would heartily approve of the mayors' actions?

I might tell Pringle, though I was beginning to think that Pringle's answer to anything was to hang or beat a few people. No, this touched upon the Stadhouder's interests, and the best that I could do was to send another letter to him. I would write one as soon as I could, but first I must make my way to Pereyra's warehouse once more. It was an overcast day, and I was not confident that we would be able to discern sunset when it came, so I had better not be late for my appointment at the synagogue.

As I made my way through the streets I caught a glimpse of that friar again; or, at least, of *a* friar. There may have been more than one, and one friar looks pretty much like another at a distance. He darted across the road and into an alleyway, emerging a little later in the street on the left of me. I also saw Father De Vroom talking to a man at a stall selling small carvings. It interested me, and as I approached I could see a splendid example of ecumenism, because on the same stall there were menorahs and crucifixes. Closer inspection revealed that on the notice affixed to the top of the cross the usual inscription INRI (an abbreviation of Jesus of Nazareth, King of the Jews) had been replaced by the name Jesus. The original might have caused offence to Jews, I suppose, and it does not do to antagonise your customers.

'Are your enquiries proceeding well, Master?' came a rich voice at my shoulder.

'Father De Vroom! I cannot say that they are, sadly. The most I can say is that no further children have disappeared thanks to the steps the Jews here have taken.'

'Yes, but it is Friday afternoon. If there is to be mischief, this is when it will be done.'

'Indeed, Father. Tell me if you will, what do you remember of the days when the other children were taken?'

De Vroom stroked his chin thoughtfully. 'Let me see. I cannot say that I remember much about the first day. It is my practice to pray before the cross of Our Lord at three o'clock on Friday afternoons, in memory of Our Lord's passion, so I must have been there, and heard nothing about it until later. The second child's mother's lamentations disturbed my prayers. I went out into the street to discover what had befallen her, and when I heard her story I joined the men searching the streets and quays.'

'Forgive my interruption,' I said, 'but is there any chance that the child could have been placed on a barge?'

'I cannot say that it was impossible, Master, but I saw no barges casting off. The canals are busy in the morning and late evening, but the only barge I saw at the quay was unloading a consignment of timber. They had not long started and would not have been ready to depart again for at least an hour. In any event, mijnheer Pereyra and his men searched through the timber in case the child had been trapped beneath.'

'And on the third day?'

'That I remember rather better. It is very recent, after all. And I know Esther Morteira too. You must realise, Master, that the Jews were not the only people who came here from Portugal. There are also Portuguese Catholics — not many, I grant, but some — and Esther and her friends include some of their old people in their food deliveries. I have been used to coming across them as I visit parishioners.'

'I was not aware that Catholics had left Portugal. Surely they were not persecuted?'

'No, but some of them were Jews who converted to Catholicism to avoid the attention of the inquisition. A portion of those have converted back to Judaism, but thus it may happen that brothers or cousins who share a business might have different religions. It makes no sense for one to stay in Portugal or Spain if his fellows have come here.'

Expressed like that, I could see his point. 'But what did you see on that day?'

'I met mevrouw Morteira as she carried bread and fish around the streets to the recipients. In fact, I met her twice, once around here and later about a block away as she returned with her empty baskets.'

'How far was she from home then?'

'Not above five minutes, I'd say.'

'But you were not in your church, so it could not have been three o'clock.'

'No, I was just about to go there. It must have been between quarter and half past two.'

'Does anyone else at your church share in your Friday observance?'

'Anyone else, Master?'

'I have seen a young Franciscan in this area. I assumed he was connected with your church.'

'There are several Franciscans who work with me.'

'I had not realised that you were yourself Franciscan.'

For answer he peeled back his cloak. 'There are laws against the display of items collected with the Roman Catholic faith. I choose not to provoke the authorities. Those who need to know my allegiance are fully aware, I assure you. If you recognised him at once as a Franciscan, I suspect you may have seen Brother Anthony Francis. I am preparing him for his ordination in due course. I cannot fault him for zeal, but I fear that he is sometimes imprudent.'

'But he does not join you for your devotions?'

'Sometimes he does, at other times not. But he does not live here, Master. He lives in one of the Order's houses and only comes to me for tuition.'

I did not dare to disclose to De Vroom that I knew exactly what he was talking about. When I was training for ordination in Namur, I lived in a seminary and visited a parish for mentorship in the pastoral side of my education.

'You must excuse me, Master — the hour of my devotions approaches,' De Vroom said, 'unless, of course, you wish to join me.'

I was about to say that I was on my way to Pereyra's warehouse and then to the synagogue, but then it occurred to me that this afforded me a wonderful opportunity to look around the secret church and, perhaps, I might persuade De Vroom to come with me to the synagogue afterwards. My chief concern was that I was supposed to be a minister of the Reformed Church, and I must not reveal any Catholic practices if we prayed together. I would have to try hard to make it look like I didn't know what I was doing.

'I should be honoured to do so, Father,' I said, 'but I must warn you that I am engaged to be at the synagogue at sunset.'

'That will present no problem,' De Vroom assured me. 'It's over three hours before sunset and my prayers, though fervent, are not that long.'

I followed him through the streets and we entered at what appeared to be an ordinary house door. Passing through a couple of rooms I found myself back in the courtyard where I had met De Vroom before. We turned in at another door and climbed some wooden steps to gain an upper room which was a rather beautiful church. De Vroom hung his cloak on a peg and we advanced to the foot of the altar, above which a crucifix was fixed to the wall.

Reformed churches do not admit of any decoration, which many of the faithful view either as superstitious or as distractions. This church would have appalled them, for not only were there multiple statuettes, but they were brightly — some would say luridly — painted. To one side I could see The Blessed Virgin Mary, to the other an image of St Anthony of Padua, for whom the church was named. There was a curious coincidence in this, because St Anthony was himself Portuguese, and renowned as the patron saint of lost things. If a Catholic has lost something, he may pray to St Anthony for its safe return. While De Vroom prayed at the foot of the cross, it would do me no harm to pray to St Anthony for the return of three lost children.

We knelt and bowed our heads. I realised that De Vroom was saying the words of the Creed. After a moment or two of silence, he continued by chanting the prayer *Salvator mundi, salva nos, qui per crucem et resurrectionem tuam liberasti nos*: Saviour of the world, save us, you who by your cross and resurrection have set us free.

Whatever came next was lost on me, because I was praying to St Anthony for a bit of help finding the Portuguese children. To be honest, this was more in hope than expectation, but if I did not get some help from somewhere I was going to achieve nothing.

I recognise that there will be readers who will put what happened next down to coincidence, but I know the hand of Providence when I see it, and I will swear that for once my prayer was answered on the spot. Well, that may be a slight exaggeration; but suddenly a thought occurred to me that I was annoyed with myself for missing. How could I have been so stupid?

I was gazing at the figure of the Blessed Virgin when a memory came to me of a painting I had seen in Antwerp, I think, but it does not really matter exactly where I saw it. It was a *virgo lactans* image, which is to say that it showed Mary feeding Jesus. Such paintings are usually antique now, because the Church has discouraged such depictions for a hundred years or more, which is perhaps why seeing one had stuck in my mind. It was only natural, after all; the infant Jesus would have needed milk.

But so did Daniel Morteira! The others might, perhaps, have managed with some sort of pap or gruel, but Daniel was too small. Moreover, I might not know much about Judaism, but I recalled that Jewish authorities expected breastfeeding at least until the age of two. There are women who experience difficulty with this and are unable to do so, but unless Esther was such a woman, if the kidnapper did not intend to harm the child he would have had to arrange a supply of milk. He would need a wet nurse.

I could barely contain my excitement until prayers concluded. When Father De Vroom at length rose to his feet, I thanked him for the pleasure of sharing in his devotions and immediately asked a highly inappropriate question.

'Father, do you know where I would find a wet nurse?'

I will grant that anyone entering the church at that moment might have been more than a little surprised to see a Reformed minister and a Catholic priest discussing wet nurses, but it was important to my enquiry.

'I don't know,' he admitted. 'There may be individuals nearby. But I'd probably ask at the Begijnhof.'

I could have kicked myself. The begijns were women who lived rather like nuns but took no vows. They could leave whenever they wanted, but quite often they were women who either did not choose to marry or who were widowed beyond childbearing age. They busied themselves in service to their area by caring for the sick, helping to deliver children and so on, and therefore they were exactly the kind of people who might be able to help you find a wet nurse. Why had I not thought of them before?

'Is the Begijnhof nearby?' I asked.

'About a mile away to the west. Is this connected to your enquiry?'

'I just thought that Daniel Morteira probably needed milk, assuming that his mother was still feeding him.'

'I'm sure she was,' De Vroom replied. 'She had started a little late that day because she was feeding Daniel. But if we go to the synagogue we can ask her.'

We strode out together and soon arrived at Pereyra's warehouse. He led us to the synagogue and arranged places for us to watch. Fortunately they had little skullcaps for both of us. Since the women had already entered their section of the synagogue we could not ask Esther, but her husband Abraham confirmed that his wife had still been feeding Daniel at the time of his disappearance, though, he lamented, her milk had now stopped flowing due to the grief of her loss.

I cannot describe exactly what happened over the next hour or so. I record only two things; that Saul Pimentel indeed had a very good voice, a fine tenor which effortlessly filled the great building, and that the Rabbi gave an address in which he urged people to help with my enquiries and to continue to safeguard their little ones. He moved between Dutch, Hebrew and another tongue that I took to be Portuguese; my Hebrew is quite restricted, being biblical Hebrew only, and his Dutch was slightly eccentric, and since I do not speak Portuguese at all my comprehension of his words may be somewhat piecemeal.

It was dark when we emerged, so I was quite relieved to see Pringle and his men waiting outside. I offered to take Pereyra and De Vroom in my carriage, but they both declined, so we parted and I braced myself for an evening of writing yet more reports.

'Where are we going?' I asked Pringle.

'To the City Hall first, Master. I believe Huydecoper is keen to speak to you.'

'Is he? Do you know what it's about?'

'Oh, yes. He wants his book back.'

CHAPTER FIFTEEN

The careful reader may have noted from my memoirs that I sometimes do not entirely grasp what is going on. I hasten to add that this does not extend to my life at the university, which is a model of order and serenity, especially when no students are around. However, these enquiries with which I become embroiled occur because something has gone wrong, and it seems to me that I am always rushing to catch up, to fill in blanks or to remember a lot of names and facts that I must suddenly learn. It is quite surprising that I ever manage to solve any of these puzzles.

On the other hand, being uninformed is occasionally useful when there are awkward questions being asked because I can truthfully give entirely unhelpful answers, and this was a case in point. Huydecoper was furious and anxious in equal measure.

'I am sorry to have to bring this up, Master, but I have reason to believe that your manservant has stolen some of my property.'

'Surely not?' I stammered.

'I am afraid so.'

'What is he accused of having taken?'

'A notebook.'

'A notebook? Why would he want a notebook? I would give him all the paper he might need.'

'I do not think he planned to write in it. I have written in it.'

'A second-hand notebook, then? Even more baffling.'

'I should be very glad if you would ask him to return it, then I will say no more about it and I will leave the matter of punishment to your judgement.'

'Why do you think he has it?' I asked. It seemed a fair question and one that an indignant master might properly ask.

'Because one of my maids has confessed to having led him to it.'

'May I question her?'

'That will not be possible. I have discharged her.'

I would gladly have handed Kees over to punishment, if I had known where he was. He had, after all, acted without any instruction from me.

'Presumably he is at mijnheer Hudde's house waiting for me,' I replied. 'I will send him here at once.'

'He is not there,' Huydecoper thundered. 'However, it is possible that my book is. By your leave, I should be grateful if you would accompany me so that we can look for it.'

I gulped. This was going to be very embarrassing. I had thought to use the book against Huydecoper, and now he was going to use its theft against me. I could imagine how my sojourn in Amsterdam was going to end when he found it under my pillow. I could hardly refuse to go with him or deny him a search, so long as it was decorous and dignified. I hurriedly pictured the contents of my travelling chest in my head in case anything in it would cause questions to be asked.

'Let us go at once,' I said, with more bravado than I was feeling.

Once there, I flung open the chamber door and invited Huydecoper and Hudde to look wherever they wished. If Huydecoper was enraged, Hudde looked like the most timid of mice hoping that a passing cat would put him out of his misery. He kept apologising to me for this unpardonable breach of hospitality, but it was clear that he was cowed by Huydecoper.

They searched the room very thoroughly and, to my relief, found nothing. The book was not there. Since I had no idea where it was, I did not blush when Huydecoper asked me if I could think where it might be and I said I could not.

'I see your servant is still not here, Master.'

'Technically,' I began, 'he is not my personal servant. He goes with the collar, loaned to me temporarily. I did not choose him, had never met him before and do not know where he is now.'

I noticed Pringle standing rigidly to attention with his single eye fixed at some point on the wall above the bed, as if looking at me might give the game away.

Hudde was trying hard to encourage Huydecoper to "see sense". 'If this book was a secret, as you say, how could the Master have had designs upon it or have played any part in its theft?' Hudde asked.

Huydecoper reluctantly agreed.

'I give you my word,' I said, 'that if Kees returns, I will send him to you with the book. But I fear he has run away.' May God forgive me the little ruse I used to draw the matter to an immediate and abrupt close. 'What was in the book anyway?' I asked.

No matter how complicated my life gets, there always seems to be something that can tangle it yet further, and quite often in those days that something was William of Orange.

Huydecoper had declined an invitation to supper and had gone home, no doubt to hurriedly write out as much of his book as he could remember, while Hudde seemed to be short of appetite, but sat with a hunk of bread and a goblet of wine, occasionally sighing or murmuring, 'Oh, dear!'

By contrast, now that I had successfully fought off the Huydecoper dragon I was ready to sup heartily. Since it was Friday, I ignored the meat and attacked a piece of cheese, explaining my preference by remarking how excellent the cheese was, and was just beginning my second goblet of wine when my appetite was sucked away by the appearance of a messenger who had, it seemed, come from William's camp. Since he had left during the afternoon, it was clear that William had moved inexorably nearer — a fact that was not lost on Hudde, who redoubled his sighing.

The messenger handed me a letter. It was sloppily sealed and had clearly been written by William personally, which explains why it took me quite a while to decipher it. If he ever sent dispatches to his ambassadors he would have had no need of code, because it is doubtful if anyone without years of practice could have read them. Our ruling pair made a contrasting couple, because Mary's handwriting was neat, though her spelling was quaintly idiosyncratic, whereas William's writing looked like a child had been let loose with a twig dipped in ink. It could be very difficult to distinguish between his l, f and t, and between his f and his s, not to mention n and v. Added to this, when he wrote personally to me he was usually in such a passion that his nib nearly ripped the page, which made his text even more angular than usual.

It told me something I did not really want to hear, namely that Kees had arrived at the camp with Huydecoper's book, which William was finding very interesting. He ensured that I would burn the letter by praising me for coming up with the idea of stealing it. I eyed the fire to check that it was still burning well so that I could rely on the paper being utterly consumed in due course.

William was delighted to hear about my conversation with Locke, which puzzled me at first, because I did not see how he had heard so quickly about it, until the realisation dawned that Kees must have taken the report with him, which in turn explained Pringle's statue act earlier, because he must have been the one who sent Kees and gave him a horse.

The Stadhouder then spent a few words giving his opinions of the mayors, which may be omitted here since the epithets used were not fitting for the memoirs of a man of the cloth. Indeed, I do not know where William learned them, unless he had been hanging around with soldiers.

He informed me that if I needed him he could be in Amsterdam in a couple of hours, but his plan was to wait until Sunday and march into the city while everyone was at Divine Service, and he would be pleased, he said, if I made a point of attending one of the churches and having a word with the minister beforehand to ensure that he did not stint on his sermon but preached for at least an hour, because it would take a while to sneak so large an army into the city. No doubt if I went there Hudde would come too, and the chances were that the mayors all worshipped in the same place anyway.

William's correspondence had one redeeming feature. Whenever he sent a secret message, he always included another one which could serve as the pretext for the letter; thus, if Hudde asked me what was in the Stadhouder's epistle I would always have something plausible to tell him (not that Hudde was ill-bred enough to ask that question). In this case, William had solved the mystery of his purpose in writing by giving me yet another job.

'The Stadhouder presents his compliments,' I said, 'and begs that while I am here I will inspect the improved defences against ice and flood.'

The previous winter of 1683-4 had been the hardest in living memory. It had been so cold that the sea had frozen. A man at Scheveningen had walked out onto the sea and kept going for nearly three hours across the ice before having to turn back, and in some of the canals the ice was so thick that a man lying on it could drill a hole deep enough to take his entire forearm without touching the water beneath. I had spent a substantial amount on a fur-lined jerkin and gloves and had still passed much of the winter sitting by the fireside.

The result of this had been that in many places the ice had pushed into the banks and quaysides and caused damage which became apparent when it melted, and the melt-water had led to disastrous floods. Fortunately, as a maritime people we know a bit about floods and you did not need to be particularly knowledgeable to realise that when huge quantities of snow and ice melt the water has to go somewhere, so even before it melted men had been employed to push the snow off the land and, in some places, into cuttings made by digging out the earth which was banked up to protect the houses behind. My job, it seemed, was to verify that Amsterdam had done this effectively, although who would think that a lecturer in moral philosophy was the right person to assess flood defences was not clear to me.

Hudde was quick to set my mind at rest. 'I should be happy to escort you on a tour of the watersides tomorrow,' he said.

That was a blow, because I really wanted to go to the Begijnhof on Saturday. There was no alternative but to say so, I thought, because honesty is always the best policy, except possibly when William asked your opinion of his latest plan. 'I was hoping to visit the Begijnhof first,' I said. 'It won't take long, but I have something I must do there.'

Hudde seemed relieved. 'That is no problem. We can make the tour in that direction, and I shall be happy to wait while you transact your business.'

I thanked him and nonchalantly tossed the letter into the fire, a carefree gesture that was rather spoiled when I had to rush to pick the burning paper up as it dropped out onto the floor. This time, I prodded it with the fire-irons until it was thoroughly incinerated, which did not stop me poking around in the ashes when Hudde left the room to check that nothing was still legible.

I was not made for this cloak-and-dagger existence.

CHAPTER SIXTEEN

You may imagine how well I slept, dear reader. In my fitful dreams small mayors were snatched from their beds by wicked begijns while Kees laughed uproariously at my inability to prevent their abduction. One pleasant aspect of this adventure had been that I had not been faced with fathers wanting me to marry their daughters, something that had bedevilled my life for quite a while. I would not have anyone think that it was my rugged and handsome appearance that provoked this behaviour, but the notion that a university man and pastor with a secure living and (presumably) no violent or adulterous tendencies might give their daughter a good life. In fact, in many congregations a minister was paid less well than a Roman Catholic priest, but if I owned up to being one of those that would make me ineligible to be a husband. At this time I was in my mid-forties, and if the death of my grandmother had reduced the pressure on me to marry, the years had also made me slightly less attractive as the potential suitor of young women, at least in the eyes of the girls. Their fathers seemed to think that the age difference was a matter of no importance whatsoever.

I mention this because when I knocked at the door of the Begijnhof, it was opened by a woman of about thirty who might have walked out of a painting. Her headwear, of course, framed her face, so I could not see her hair, but she had a pleasing oval face, blonde eyebrows and beautiful oval green eyes. Her skin was smooth and had a blush like a ripe peach, and when she saw that a man was in front of her she dropped her eyes in the most demure way that I found utterly enchanting.

Needless to say, I completely forgot why I had come for a moment.

'I am sorry to disturb you,' I said at last. 'I am Master Mercurius of the University of Leiden, here at the command of the Stadhouder, and I should be grateful for a few minutes' conversation with whoever is in charge.'

'If you will step inside, Master, I will see if our Mistress can see you.'

Her voice was surprisingly deep for such a delicate frame. I found myself thinking that if she sang as she spoke she must be a pleasing contralto.

She led the way along a path to a large room in the corner, where she invited me to sit on a bench while she went in search of the Mistress. This took very little time and soon I was springing to my feet to introduce myself to Mistress Agnes.

Mistress Agnes was not delicate, green-eyed or graceful. She looked like a milkmaid, which was not unfitting given that she apologised for the fact that her hand had just been inserted in a cow. I did not enquire why; no doubt she had her reasons. She had a pleasant smile, a snub nose and two dark eyes as if someone had pushed small coals into her face.

'I am grateful to you for seeing me,' I said. 'I am investigating the disappearance of three Portuguese children who have been abducted elsewhere in the city. I have been trying to think where they might have been taken.'

'Not here, I assure you,' Mistress Agnes replied. 'It is true that sometimes mothers abandon children here, but if anyone brings a child we ask where they have come from. We much prefer to support a mother to keep her child than that she should abandon it.'

'These children are not abandoned, but stolen,' I replied.

'And recently so, or you would not be asking about them, but we have not received a child here for over a year, nor, to the best of my knowledge, has anyone asked us to do so.' She turned to the woman who had opened the door and arched an eyebrow in mute interrogation.

'That is so,' agreed the doorkeeper.

'And Jutte would know, because she always answers the door.'

Jutte! What a pretty name, I thought. She had a certain calmness and confidence that came from being completely self-contained, I thought, not like these young girls I had met in the past.

'I do not think a woman would have brought the children. Indeed, their mothers would not, because they were in such distress over their loss,' I explained. 'Nor do I suppose that the children were brought here. But I wonder whether anyone has approached you asking if you know of a wet nurse.'

The two women looked at each other, but their expressions were not identical. Mistress Agnes appeared puzzled, as if she could not think why anyone would do such a thing, whereas Jutte seemed to be debating whether she should say something.

'What an extraordinary question! Why would someone expect to find a wet nurse here?' Mistress Agnes asked.

'I doubt very much that they did,' I replied. 'But I think that they may have had nowhere else to make enquiries because they needed a wet nurse urgently and they thought you might know. This would have been on the Friday after Easter.'

Jutte gasped and covered her mouth with her hand in shock.

'Mistress Agnes, may I ask what mevrouw Jutte knows?' I asked.

'Jutte, if you know something, you must speak,' said Mistress Agnes.

Jutte still appeared reluctant to say anything, so I felt I should encourage her.

'These three children, all under three years old, were stolen from their mothers. We believe the kidnapper needed a wet nurse for at least one of them, and probably had not thought beforehand that one would be needed, so he would have just a couple of hours to find one before the babe needed feeding.'

'Someone did enquire,' Jutte replied, 'but not on that Friday.'

'No?' I said.

'No, Master. It was on the previous Saturday.'

'I see. And did you give him a suggestion?'

'May God forgive me, I did,' answered Jutte, who was by now close to tears at the thought that she might inadvertently have assisted in the separation of a child from his mother.

'You cannot have known that his intentions were evil,' I said, 'and therefore I cannot see why you would need forgiveness.'

'Mistress Agnes, I sent him to see Aletta Brouwer.'

The name meant nothing to me, but it plainly did to Mistress Agnes, who nodded slowly. 'That was sensible of you.' She turned to me to explain. 'Aletta is a local woman whose husband died before their baby was born. She came to us to seek alms to keep herself alive, having no income after his passing and no family to support her and her child.'

'I see. Then I have two further questions. Where can I find Aletta?'

'Very close, Master,' said Jutte. 'She lives in a hut behind the bakery opposite.'

'Thank you. I will speak to her, and I will give her some charity in her loss. Now to my second question — do you know the man who asked you for a wet nurse?'

'No, Master,' said Jutte. 'I wish I did, but I am afraid I had never seen him before and I have not seen him since.'

I was disappointed, but perhaps all was not lost. 'Would you recognise him if you saw him again?'

'I'm not sure, Master. He wore a large cloak and his hood was up. But I would be happy to try.'

As I left, I noticed Mistress Agnes comforting Jutte. If I had realised comfort was needed, I would have done that.

I felt guilty about making Hudde wait, but I thought it was important that I should follow every clue as quickly as might be. In the event, Hudde volunteered to come with me, so together we crossed the street to the bakery and found the narrow path that led to the hut behind it.

It was hardly a house. Indeed, when it was first erected I am sure it was never intended that anyone should live in it, for it was less than three paces across. There was a small table, a chair of sorts with a large crack in the top rail, and a straw mattress rolled up in one corner. A baby gurgled in a basket while mevrouw Brouwer lifted a turnip out of a pan of hot water.

We introduced ourselves and I explained why we had come.

'Mevrouw, we understand that a man asked at the begijnhof for the name of a wet nurse and was given your name. I wonder whether he came to speak to you. This would be at Easter or a day or two later.'

Aletta bit her lip in uncertainty. 'Forgive me, but may I eat my food while it's hot? I could share it if…'

'No, thank you. Please eat it yourself.'

There was nowhere near enough to share. If this was her meal for the day, how was she keeping body and soul together? She picked the turnip up in her hands and began to nibble at it.

'A man came, yes, on a Saturday. He asked if I would be prepared to feed a baby for him. I said I would. I would have done it for any baby in need if I could, but he offered me two stuivers for a feed.'

'And did he bring the baby to you?'

'Yes, on the following Friday, late in the afternoon. It was almost dark.'

'And how long was the baby with you?'

'No more than an hour, Master. I fed him once while the man waited outside, and then he took him away again. He said he was on a journey to the child's mother but it would take too long to leave the child without milk.'

'Can you describe the child?'

'It was a big boy, Master. I had expected an infant, but this child was about a year old, I'd say. He had teeth,' she said ruefully.

'And how was he dressed?'

'Why, in baby clothes.'

'I mean, did he look like he came from a rich family or a poor one?'

'His clothes were better than I can give my Jacob, but not fine. I had to clean him.' She stopped speaking and blushed.

'Yes?' I prompted.

'Well, he wasn't like Jacob. His … you know. It was different.'

As an exchange of information this lacked something, because she could not explain herself and I did not realise at first what she meant, then it came to me. I suppose most Dutch women would not have seen a circumcised man.

'That sounds very like one of the children we're looking for. Tell me about the man who came.'

Aletta thought hard but shook her head. 'The first time he came he had a cloak and hood, so I did not see him clearly. He had a sharp nose, I noticed, and no beard. But the second time it was growing dark and I have little light here.'

I could not see a candle at all. She must have worked by daylight and slept as soon as night fell. 'Was he a young man?'

'I think so, Master.'

'And how tall?'

She considered. 'Maybe a little taller than you.'

I reached into my pouch and found some coins for her. 'Thank you,' I said. 'You've been very helpful.'

She inspected her palm and thanked me. I was embarrassed that she was so grateful for so little. It would relieve her for a few days, and then she would return to her meagre life. I turned to go, but out of the corner of my eye I saw Hudde push a single coin into her hand. Her eyes opened wide as she saw what he had given her. I am not sure what it was, but it was a large piece of silver.

We thanked her and stepped outside. I was waiting for Hudde to adjust his hat when the door opened again and she ran out and grabbed my arm.

'I remembered something,' she said. 'Maybe it will help, maybe it won't.'

'Please speak,' I said earnestly.

'His shoes. I remember thinking that it was very cold to be wearing those shoes.'

When she explained what she meant, I did not immediately understand the importance of what she was telling me, but in a little while I understood entirely. Not only that, but I had an idea about the whole case, though I could not see how to bring it to a happy conclusion.

We returned to the carriage and I sat in thought.

'Are you any wiser, Master?' asked Hudde.

'How could I not be, since I have obviously been such a blockhead hitherto?' I answered him.

It was true. Now that I had this clue, so many things became clearer to me, and many were so obvious that I thought myself the greatest fool alive to have missed them before. I did not have a motive, but at least I could see how the thing had been done, and a suspicion that I had formed about the removal of Daniel Morteira from his crib had now crystallised into a definite sequence of events that I could see clearly.

'You know, then, who is responsible?'

'Yes,' I said sadly, 'I think I do. I just hope he was working alone.'

Hudde gazed absently out of the window and spoke quietly. 'Master, if that is so, then it seems to me that the inspection of the canal defences is unimportant.'

'Try telling that to the Stadhouder.'

'Oh, I think that if we both say so he will not argue with us. He is not an unreasonable man.'

I weighed up the evidence for and against that proposition without being able to reach a definite conclusion. Given that William had specifically directed me to conduct such an inspection, albeit as a cover for his other instructions, I was reluctant not to carry it through, but I took some comfort from Hudde's support; and surely finding missing children must be more important than anything else that I could do. I hoped my suppositions about the culprit were right, because if they were then there was every reason to believe that the children would be alive and well cared for, but there was always the chance that I might be wrong. I had been wrong before; not often, admittedly, but to discount the possibility would be rank arrogance.

'Then let us see if we can find him,' I said, and gave instructions to the coachman. As we travelled through the streets I explained my notions to Hudde, who was shocked at my conclusions but did not dispute them. However, he observed that I had very little in the way of evidence.

I was emboldened by the episode with the card players. If I lacked evidence, perhaps I could bluff the culprit into providing it for me. If I gave the impression that I knew more than I did I might even get a confession, or, if not an overt confession, maybe the villain would attempt to run away, which would be as good as a confession.

We came to a halt and alighted from the carriage. Pringle and his men had fallen in behind us and Pringle dismounted, presumably perplexed by our change of plan.

'Our quarry may not be here,' I explained, 'but if he is, I'd like to know that he cannot escape through the back door.'

Pringle smiled grimly. 'I'll make sure he can't escape through any door, Master.'

'And if he isn't there, we must make sure that nobody warns him. He is the only person who can tell us where the children are.'

Pringle considered this briefly. 'Then if he is not there, please tell us and my men will retreat out of sight so that we do not frighten him off.'

Having thus made our plan, Hudde and I knocked at the door while Pringle went to deploy his men. After a few moments a servant appeared.

'We would like to see Father De Vroom,' I said. 'It is a matter of some urgency.'

'I'll see if he will see you,' said the servant.

'I'm sure he will find it convenient to do so,' Hudde added. 'And if he doesn't, ask him again. We will wait inside.' So saying, he pushed past the servant and entered the hall.

This was a side of Hudde I had not seen before. Suddenly I could understand how he could have become a man of such prominence in his community. He had not always been a tentative, nervous, cautious man.

Father de Vroom descended to greet us, a grave expression on his face. He knew Hudde by reputation, if not by appearance, and seemed to prefer to address him rather than me until Hudde made it plain that I was going to ask the questions.

'The Master and I have been to the Begijnhof today, as a result of which he has some questions to ask,' said Hudde.

De Vroom turned to me. I think I detected a scowl being suppressed.

'Father, where is Brother Anthony Francis?'

'He is within.'

'Would you lead us to him, please?'

'May I ask why?'

I wanted to ensure that Brother Anthony Francis did not escape us, so I was quite sharp. 'I will explain when he is with us, Father.'

We mounted the stairs and found the Brother at prayer. We waited for him to notice us and bring his prayers to an end which, in due time, he did, though I suspected that he had seen us and was thinking about what he was going to say.

'These gentlemen wish to speak to you, Brother,' De Vroom announced.

'Me, Father? What business can they have with me?'

He stepped towards us, and as the light fell on him I could see a young man, spare of frame. He was tonsured, but I think his hair would have been receding anyway. His grey eyes displayed intelligence, and his face was completed with high cheekbones, a narrow chin and a straight, sharp nose.

'I have been engaged by the Stadhouder to investigate the disappearance of three Portuguese children,' I began.

'I heard that they were missing,' he replied.

'I do not think that you needed to be told,' I said. 'We have been to the Begijnhof where a person whose description closely matches your appearance asked for the services of a wet nurse before the smallest child was taken, as if in anticipation of a need.'

Anthony Francis sniffed. 'There must be many men of my general appearance.'

'Indeed there are,' I agreed, 'but there are not that many who habitually wear sandals.'

Now he looked rather more concerned.

'You see,' I continued, 'I was unable to think how the children could vanish so completely so quickly, but then I realised that there are many alleyways in this district. The difficulty is that not all of them have an exit. You would need some local knowledge to be aware of those that act as shortcuts, which is interesting because that is exactly what the kidnapper did. Even then, the children's disappearance was noticed swiftly and the area was soon closed off for a search. Somehow he managed to sneak the children out of the district without using the main streets. That puzzled me for a while, but now I realise that we are standing in the best place to make an explanation, aren't we? The child was brought into this complex of buildings and moved to the far side through the connected houses, finally coming out on the street to the far side. That enabled you to keep ahead of the searchers, Brother Anthony Francis. And I know you know about the alleyways because I saw you using them the other day.'

De Vroom was nonplussed. 'Is this true, Brother? Aren't you going to deny it?'

'I have nothing to say to these wild allegations,' Anthony Francis said calmly.

'Well, let me add further "wild allegations" to the catalogue,' I continued, rather cross at his refusal to acknowledge his sin.

'Master Mercurius,' Hudde interrupted, 'would it not be wiser to take Brother Anthony Francis and Father De Vroom to the City Hall so that all the mayors can hear what is said? It will avoid the need to repeat yourself later.'

CHAPTER SEVENTEEN

We drew up in front of the City Hall and Hudde went to summon all the mayors. Geelvinck was already there, and the others arrived within a few minutes. We assembled in an upper chamber and Pringle arranged guards at all the doors. The four mayors sat behind a long table while Father De Vroom was given a chair. Brother Anthony Francis and I stood to speak.

'Let me remind you of the basic facts as we know them,' I began. 'Isidore de Espinosa disappeared from a courtyard behind his parents' house. Despite suggestions to the contrary, he cannot have opened the gate to let himself out because he could not reach the latch; and if he had stood on something to do so, the door would not have opened inwards. However, I have visited the courtyard and satisfied myself that an adult standing outside could see through the fence to verify that the child was present and that no adult was immediately to hand. You see, these were not opportunistic abductions. The perpetrator wanted these particular children for some reason. Jewish boys less than three years old were his quarry.'

'Let us hope that whoever it was he used them better than King Herod used the infant boys in Bethlehem,' Huydecoper remarked.

'Indeed,' I agreed. 'Let us hope so. Having abducted the boy, Brother Anthony Francis proceeded through the alleyway and across the street, turning in at the Moses and Aaron Church and running through the connected buildings to the far side. I need hardly say that Father De Vroom knew nothing of this.'

'One moment,' said Hudde. 'We ought at least to formally ask the question.'

De Vroom stood briefly. 'I give you my word that I did not. I have worked many years in that quarter and made many friendships. I would never have jeopardised them in this way.'

He resumed his seat. I think that we were all convinced of his sincerity, but I was kicking myself that I had been prepared to take his innocence for granted. What else had I got wrong?

'Once outside the district, Brother Anthony Francis could take his time conducting the child to wherever he planned to take him. The second child to disappear was Shmuel Pimentel, taken from the doorstep of his house. His mother was gone for just a few moments, but it was enough for a fit young man to scoop the boy up and turn the nearest corner. I wondered how this could be done, but then I realised that Rachel Pimentel may have searched in both directions, but she cannot have searched them both simultaneously. Like any mother, her first thought would be to look in the direction that posed most danger, so she would head towards the bend in the road, beyond which her child would be out of sight. In fact, Brother Anthony Francis was concealed in a doorway in the other direction until her back was turned. If she had run that way, he would doubtless have handed the child over claiming to have seen him unattended. Having gained the corner, he would be able to use lanes and alleys to get to the church and then emerge far away from the scene of the crime.'

'You have no proof for this,' Anthony Francis alleged.

'Let me describe the third case, and then we will see whether I have proof. Daniel Morteira was in a crib in his house. He was being watched by his father while his mother was engaged in charitable work. I believe Father De Vroom knows of the help that she extends to the elderly of any faith in the district.'

De Vroom nodded to confirm that it was so.

'When Abraham Morteira heard his wife return, he moved the crib nearer the back door, into the part of the kitchen where his wife usually worked. By his account his wife came to him some minutes later to say that the child was missing. However, his wife says that she noticed their loss immediately on her return. At first I assumed that she was overwrought and misremembering, but then I found myself thinking that we should not make such sloppy assumptions. Was there a way in which both could be right?

'The answer is not exactly. But both were honest witnesses. The thing to note is that Abraham heard his wife return; he did not say he saw her. He assumed the person entering the house was Esther because he was expecting her. He may even have heard the swish of a dress along the floor. But in fact it was not a woman he heard, but a friar. You knew Esther Morteira was out, and that therefore Abraham might be caring for him while also trying to work, with all the attendant distractions he would have, so you sneaked in at the rear but then realised that Abraham was round the corner in his work area. In haste you stepped into their parlour. It was while you were there that Abraham brought the crib out, so when he returned to his workshop you grabbed the boy and ran.'

Anthony Francis gave me a pitying look. 'And why would I do that?' he asked.

I did not know. Was he one of those tormented souls who enjoys destroying children? Did he hate Jews so much that he wanted to kill their first-born sons? Our eyes met, his blazing with contempt, mine pained by what I had to say; and somehow an idea flashed into my head. 'You gave them to Christian families.'

His eyes flicked away, and I knew then that I was right.

'You took Jewish children, and gave them to Christians to bring up as their own,' I continued. 'That is why they had to be boys. Which childless couple wants a girl? And even if common gossips noticed that a previously barren woman had a surprisingly old child, it could be passed off as an act of charity, giving a home to an orphan; except that they were not orphans, were they? They had grieving mothers and fathers. Jews are no different to us. If we prick them, they bleed; if we tickle them, they laugh; and if we steal their children, they cry.'

De Vroom was furious. 'Is this true?' he boomed. 'Have you fallen thus far into sin?'

There was no reply.

'They had to be small children,' I went on, 'who would retain no memories of their earlier life. In time they would come to believe that these couples had always been their parents. The particular problem with Daniel Morteira, which I suspect you had not realised when you earmarked him for abduction, was that he was still being fed by his mother. You had to ensure that you had someone standing by to feed him because these children were being sent to families a long way from here, so that there would be no chance that they would be discovered by chance, and the infant would need feeding during that time. I imagine they now live somewhere near another Franciscan house. Anyway, you asked at the Begijnhof for the name of a wet nurse, and the woman you were sent to remembered that you wore sandals — a very unusual choice of footwear in the filthy streets of Amsterdam. She could not, of course, see your clothing or tonsure, but she did look at your feet. And it is your footwear that condemns you.'

I fell silent and waited, but there was no reply.

'Well,' Huydecoper asked, 'have you nothing to say in your defence?'

'Why do I need to defend myself?' the friar spat defiantly. 'I have saved three souls. We are called upon to convert Jews and I have done so. Six Christian men and women now have a son to love and bring up as a good Christian. Why must I defend that?'

'You scoundrel!' De Vroom shouted. 'You serpent! I have taken you under my wing. I introduced you to these people. I never thought to be repaid with such villainy. I cannot face them again now. I must ask to be assigned elsewhere. The work of many years lies in tatters because you took it upon yourself to act as God's agent in these unholy acts.'

'I thought we were all God's agents,' snapped Brother Anthony Francis. 'Isn't that the point of our profession?'

I had never seen a clergyman hit another before. From time to time at synods I have been sorely tempted, but then I have not been moved as strongly as Father De Vroom was moved in that moment. His hand shot out and slapped the friar stingingly on the cheek.

'May God forgive you!' he exclaimed. 'And may He instruct me how to forgive, because I find myself unable to do so at present.'

Huydecoper took the mayors to a corner to confer. Since the villain had confessed, they could, as the local civic powers, proceed directly to sentence in accordance with the law, and then have it carried out. The Stadhouder did not intervene in such cases, and his judges were fully occupied in trying cases where the crime was denied.

After a few minutes they resumed their seats. Pringle had, meanwhile, taken the precaution of securing the friar's hands with rope.

'Brother Anthony Francis,' Huydecoper pronounced, 'you have admitted the abduction of these three babes. The sentence for kidnapping is death. We might mitigate it if you assist us in recovering these children and restoring them to their parents.'

'I am not afraid of martyrdom,' the friar declared. 'I know I shall be rewarded in Heaven.'

This time it was Huydecoper who slapped him. 'You dare to speak of entering Heaven? If I know my Bible, there will be no place for the likes of you there. What say you, Master?'

I should have preferred not to be asked. As a good Calvinist I know that God is very fussy about whom he admits to His presence, and that only the elect can hope to be retained at His side. On the other hand, as a Catholic I can believe that salvation is open to all who truly repent of their sins and that we can never know the likelihood that anyone else will be saved.

'I think,' I stuttered, 'that I have doubts about my own admission to Heaven sometimes, and I haven't stolen three babies. If God is prepared to overlook that, I have misunderstood His nature all this while.'

Huydecoper seemed satisfied by my response. He stood close to Brother Anthony Francis and fixed him with a fierce gaze. 'You needn't think your execution will go easily for you. If you do not produce the children safe and well, we must presume them to be dead, and as a child murderer you can expect no mercy from us. You will hang, but only for a while. Then the executioner will cut you down and lie you on a table. He'll emasculate you publicly — one clean sweep of his knife, and he'll display your privities to the crowd before forcing them into your mouth. And then he'll proceed to disembowel you. I'll tell him not to rush that part. I wouldn't want you to blink and miss any of it.'

The friar did not flinch, though his mouth seemed to have become rather dry.

'Then we'll have you dismembered and your body burned. How will you be resurrected then when the last trumpet sounds?'

'God can provide me a new, more glorious body,' the friar maintained.

'Perhaps,' agreed Huydecoper. 'With new, more glorious private parts. But perhaps He won't.'

De Vroom interrupted. His tone had changed now. 'The future of your soul is no small thing, Brother!' he exclaimed. 'If you will not admit that what you have done is sinful, you cannot repent; and if you cannot repent, you cannot be admitted to Paradise.'

'Where in this is my sin?' asked Anthony Francis.

I would have admired his steadfastness were I not bamboozled by his utter stupidity.

'Take him away!' Huydecoper yelled. 'He will die in three days.'

The friar appeared unconcerned. 'May I be visited by a priest to hear my final confession?' he asked.

'I can't absolve you...' began De Vroom.

'Some other priest,' the friar explained.

CHAPTER EIGHTEEN

'The trouble with executing him,' I said, 'is that then we will never know what happened to the children.'

'Do you think I don't know that, Master?' Huydecoper hissed. 'But as his execution looms nearer, perhaps the approaching terrors may cause him to think again. There's nothing like watching your scaffold being built to concentrate a man's thoughts.'

'There may be an alternative,' I mused, 'but it will require you to trust me with your prisoner. I can think of one person who might be able to loosen the Brother's stubborn tongue.'

'If you can do that, then the city of Amsterdam will be in your debt,' Hudde said.

'If one of you wishes to accompany me, I shall be glad to have you there,' I added.

Geelvinck and Van Beuningen pleaded their business affairs kept them fully occupied. To my relief Huydecoper proposed that Hudde should go, and Hudde agreed.

'We'll leave after Divine Service tomorrow,' I said.

'On a Sunday?' Hudde exclaimed in surprise.

'Certainly,' I said. 'It's the one day of the week when I know exactly where he will be.'

Pringle had surpassed himself. I had not relished the thought of so long a journey with the errant friar in the carriage, but he had managed to find a large metal cage previously used for some wild animal and overnight some workmen secured it to a cart. It seemed that money could always be found for some things.

Brother Anthony Francis was brought out and installed in the cage.

'I hope it doesn't rain,' I said, 'since he has no protection against the elements.'

'That's very Christian of you, Master,' said Pringle. 'I'm not sure I care too much about that.'

I climbed inside the carriage and settled myself into my place. I was getting quite used to this now. There was a tap at the window, where I noticed Pringle looking in.

'It would help considerably, Master, if you would tell us where we're going,' he explained.

'Utrecht, Captain,' I answered.

'We'd better step it out, then. That's a good six hours away.'

He gave the command to move out, and our party processed from the City Hall. Once again the local populace treated my passing with indifference, with the exception of one old hag who shouted that it was a good thing that I was going and that Hudde could go to hell too. I feared that Pringle might slash her with his sword, but he told me later that he judged this to be fair comment on a matter of public interest, so he left her alone.

A long journey by carriage is not that enjoyable. Those in the carriage quickly run out of things to say to each other, and since it was a Sunday there was very little to comment on in the villages we passed through. Hudde had the foresight to have tucked a little book in his pocket, whereas I passed much of the time inspecting the inside of my eyelids.

We turned in to Utrecht late in the afternoon, and I asked the watchkeepers on the city gate for directions to the Roman Catholic Chapel. Utrecht has a substantial Catholic population and it was only twelve years since the French had restored Catholic services in the Dom during their occupation, so I was taken aback when the guard tried to tell me that there were no Catholic churches in the city.

I showed him the badge hanging from my collar. 'I am here on the Stadhouder's official business,' I said.

'Oh!' he grinned. 'You've come to close them down! Well, I suppose I'll have to tell you where they are, then.'

He directed us first to St Gertrude's Chapel, which is hard against the canal to the west side of the city. As he suspected, this is where I could find Johannes van Neercassel.

I hesitate to burden the reader with more history than is necessary, but a little explanation may help. When the United Provinces gained their independence from Spain the Catholic Church lost many privileges and some of its dignitaries fled. Punitive laws were enacted which, as I have remarked earlier, remain in force. The hierarchy disappeared and the Netherlands lost its bishops. Instead, the Church was reduced to a *Missio Hollandica*, a Dutch Mission, headed by a Vicar Apostolic, who, at this time, was Van Neercassel. In all but name he was Archbishop of Utrecht.

Van Neercassel was keen to improve the standing of the Church but knew that this would only be possible if everyone kept to the informal rules that prevented the penal laws from being enforced. Thus the churches — including his own chapel — looked like ordinary houses and the Catholic clergy walked the streets in plain drab clothes rather than displaying their status.

I had never met him, and I hoped that he was unaware of my existence. He made a point of interviewing every Dutch graduate of the seminary at Louvain in the southern provinces, and therefore knew many of the priests in his own country, and he probably knew that there were others who had been secretly ordained like me, though he would not know their names. I was relying on this for the bluff that I had in mind, but it would all come horribly unstuck if it proved that he knew of my secret ordination, in which event there would be two in the cage for the return journey.

It was no surprise that Van Neercassel agreed to see me. He would not dare to slight an emissary from the Stadhouder. His superiors at the Vatican believed that he was occasionally too accommodating to the Stadhouder's whims, but by being so he had stayed in post for over twenty years and had secured some relaxation of the rules for Catholics.

When we entered he rose to meet us. There was no grandeur here, no hint that we were in the presence of the head of the Catholic Church in our land. I introduced Hudde and De Vroom, and Pringle and some of his men brought Brother Anthony Francis forward, forcing him to his knees in front of Van Neercassel.

'Your name, Brother?' he asked.

'Anthony Francis.'

There was a presence about Van Neercassel that was unmistakable. He spoke slowly, with pauses between his sentences, but this simply gave the impression of a man at peace. Languidly he raised his eyes from the prostrate figure at his feet to gaze into mine. 'Why do you bring this man here, Master?' he asked quietly.

'He has admitted to kidnapping Jewish children and giving them to Christian families to be brought up in the Catholic faith,' I explained. 'For this, the authorities at Amsterdam have sentenced him to be executed on Wednesday morning. His activities, undoubtedly unsanctioned, have caused some embarrassment to Father De Vroom, who lives among these families. It is of the highest importance that those children are returned to their parents, but Brother Anthony Francis refuses to say where they have been taken. Once he is executed, those children are lost to their parents forever.'

'I see,' Van Neercassel said with a frown. 'But I do not understand my part in this tragedy.'

'You can imagine the damage this episode will do to the Catholic Church when the sentence is carried out and it is generally known that the children were abducted by a Catholic religious.'

De Vroom added his plea. 'This man is to be hanged, drawn and quartered. He says that he is willing to suffer martyrdom in exchange for having brought the Holy Church three new souls. But when the Jews hear of this, they will tear my church down and undo my years of work there. Despite this, his pride tells him that God will not punish him for these acts, but rather reward him with a place in Paradise.'

Van Neercassel reached down and tilted Brother Anthony Francis's head upwards. 'Is this so, my son?'

'I am not afraid of a martyr's death,' the obstinate friar exclaimed.

Van Neercassel invited us all to sit — except the miserable Franciscan on his knees. 'At the risk of repeating my question, what do you want me to do? His superior is the General Minister of his Order. I have limited authority over him. I can ban him from working in the area under my control, but since you plan to end his life on Wednesday I cannot see that such a ban would have much point.'

'All that is true,' I answered, 'but you are a man of learning and experience. As a minister in the Reformed Church, I would not presume to speak definitively on the matter, but I question whether he will be received with honour in Heaven following such sins.'

I did not dare to say that I would not be asking the question if I had not been absolutely certain of the answer; but it was important the Brother should hear it from the highest authority in the Catholic Church in our country rather than from me. He would laugh at my opinion, and I could not reveal my credentials as a priest of the Catholic Church. I just hoped I had not given myself away to this astute prelate in front of me.

'The judgments of the Almighty are His alone to make,' Van Neercassel replied, 'but such kidnapping can be viewed as the most heinous species of theft. And I am sure that in your religion as in mine, the same Ten Commandments apply, one of which is to forbid stealing.'

'Then there will be consequences of such an action?'

'You have already said that there will, for he is to forfeit his life.'

'His life might yet be spared if those children are found and restored.'

'I do not wish it to be spared!' Anthony Francis declared. 'I am not ashamed of what I have done. It was done for the greater glory of the Holy Catholic and Apostolic Church.'

Don't get me wrong — I am as keen on religion as any man. That is why I have been ordained twice. But I am not a fanatic about it like this fellow, and frankly such vehemence leaves me feeling rather uneasy. It is on a par with those men who publicly scourge themselves with little whips on certain Church holy days, which all seems a shade exhibitionist to me. Mortification of the flesh is not my thing. I think that eating Albrecht's cooking is about as far as I like to go in that direction. And, I suppose, keeping my vow of celibacy despite temptations; not that any woman has tried to tempt me, but their fathers often have, and my nature is too susceptible to a pretty woman. I have never fallen, but I have tottered once or twice. That reminded me that it would be pleasant to say goodbye to Jutte before I left Amsterdam, for good, I hoped.

This train of thought was rudely interrupted by Van Neercassel's voice. This was a man who could make himself heard in the largest church, so when he decided to speak fortissimo in a small chamber with brick walls you can imagine that it was quite startling.

'Have you learned nothing in your studies?' he thundered at Brother Anthony Francis, who would have stepped back had he been on his feet rather than his knees. 'Do you suppose that Almighty God will admit an unrepentant thief to Heaven? Consider the very words of Our Lord on the Cross which were directed to the penitent thief beside him: "This day thou shalt be with me in Paradise." Our Lord said no such thing to the unrepentant sinner hanging on his other side. From which I take it that the unhappy fellow was not to see the wonders of Heaven, but rather to pass eternity in the fires of Hell. Is that what you want?'

'I was serving the Church,' protested Anthony Francis.

'You dare to accuse Holy Mother Church of soliciting such vile activity?' Van Neercassel yelled. Somehow he had found another level of volume which was highly impressive, if deafening. I did not like to interrupt to point out that, as a matter of fact, the Catholic Church had approved the forcible conversion of infants on several occasions in the past and would no doubt do so again. It seemed impolite to contradict a Church dignitary.

'We are commanded in the gospel to make disciples of all nations,' Anthony Francis doggedly persisted.

'By persuasion of the adult mind, not by indoctrination of the infant one. There is no merit accruing to your soul in these acts, no countervailing benefit to offset the evil that you have done in separating a babe from their parents.'

'Their new parents will love them and can provide well for them.'

Van Neercassel cranked the volume up once more. It was like being trapped in a small privy with a large soprano; not that such a thing has ever happened to me, but you know what I mean. 'You dare to attempt to justify your sin with such considerations? If Almighty God made their parents poor, that is because such is their station in life. Who are you to interfere with that?' Van Neercassel strode forward and lifted the unfortunate friar's chin. 'I have had my doubts about many men, but never before have I been so sure that I am looking into the face of a damned man.'

'Do not say that!' pleaded Anthony Francis.

'I say only the truth. I can say no other.'

Anthony Francis began to weep, as anyone would who had just been told by an expert that an eternity in Hell awaited them. It would spoil anyone's afternoon to hear such news.

'There is only one hope for you. You must repent of your sins. And in order to repent, you must first accept that what you have done is wrong. Next you must compensate for it, undoing the evil so far as you are able. Finally, you must undertake not to do it again — though since they're executing you on Wednesday we may take that for granted.'

Brother Anthony Francis continued to weep, having thrown himself to the floor.

'I believe,' I prompted, 'that the Brother will need to make his confession. If you will hear it, we will wait outside. But I trust that any meaningful confession will include disclosure of the whereabouts of the children, and that this will not be given under the confessional veil of secrecy.'

I was concerned that anything said in the act of confession cannot be revealed by the priest, though he may — and will — encourage the malefactor to repeat the confession to the proper authorities.

'I should not like to have to advise the Stadhouder that the Catholic Church was a threat to the children of his subjects and that therefore the penal laws should be rigidly enforced and, indeed, strengthened,' I said.

Van Neercassel was shocked. He had done my bidding in this matter, but I wanted to remind him that without the return of the children he would have achieved nothing. I admit that my words were brutal, but the stakes were very high; and while William had not empowered me to make such a threat, Van Neercassel was not to know that. On the face of it, I had the delegated power to close all the Catholic churches in the land and have all the priests conducted to the border of the country and expelled, if not worse. He had not manoeuvred his Church with great skill for over twenty years to see the Dutch Mission forcibly closed now. As I suspected, he took the threat very seriously.

'There is more than your miserable soul at stake here,' he snarled at Anthony Francis. 'Do you see now what your meddling has done?'

I bowed to the Vicar Apostolic and led our little party outside to give the penitent and his confessor some privacy. I had no doubt that whatever penance Van Neercassel imposed, it would be a very heavy one.

CHAPTER NINETEEN

An hour passed. A servant kindly brought us some wine and small cakes, which were very welcome since we had not stopped to eat earlier, and a brazier was brought to warm the room.

I realise that many of my readers will not have travelled in a carriage, so permit me to explain that while it is more comfortable than walking, it is very hard on the rear end. In my experience the constant jolting is likely to cause some intestinal disorder, and a few long journeys in the carriage had already left my insides in confusion. The reduced opportunities for refreshment had left me very constipated and I was not looking forward to the journey back, especially since we would be making it in the dark, though the attendance of a company of armed soldiers made that less of a worry than it might normally have been. The United Provinces is not an especially lawless country, but a man travelling alone from Utrecht to Amsterdam during the night might never arrive.

I was beginning to think of finding an inn for us when the door opened and Van Neercassel emerged. He held out his hand, in which there was a folded piece of paper. 'Three names and three addresses,' he remarked simply.

'Thank you,' I replied. 'If we are able to retrieve the infants, it may go some way towards reducing his punishment.'

'Really?' said Van Neercassel. 'He remains a miscreant.'

'If God can forgive, then surely we must try to do so,' I answered.

'Perhaps; but a state that pardons its criminals will find them flocking here from all parts of Christendom. It cannot be good policy.' Van Neercassel glanced out of the window. 'It is dark. I doubt that you will return tonight. Have you arranged accommodation?'

'We have not,' I admitted. 'I did not know how long this would take.'

'You are welcome to stay here,' Van Neercassel said. 'It is not palatial, but we have beds. Please be my guests for supper.'

'What of the prisoner?' asked Hudde.

'He can spend the night in his cage,' Pringle answered.

'I think,' said Van Neercassel, 'that he would be better employed in a vigil of prayer for his soul here in the chapel.'

We followed him into the chapel, dragging the unfortunate friar behind us. Now that he had been brought to realise that he had forfeited his life to no good end, he seemed to have lost the power of perambulation, not to mention being rather unhappy.

'Stop sobbing!' Pringle ordered. 'I hope you're not going to make a fuss like this on Wednesday while they disembowel you.'

This did not seem to me to be the right thing to say in the circumstances. Goodness knows that my dear mother used to say that I had never learned tact, but I think even I knew that a man who is shortly to be launched into eternity in several parts may not wish to be reminded of the prospect. In fact, I did not want to be reminded of it myself, and I sincerely hoped that I would not be expected to stay for the spectacle.

Brother Anthony Francis was secured to a pillar by a chain, and a couple of guards left to watch over him.

'If he tries to escape, do your best not to kill him,' Pringle warned them. 'We don't want him to have a quick death here. And if he dies here, the burghers of Amsterdam may feel that they don't want a perfectly good scaffold to go to waste.'

The soldiers involuntarily checked their necks for invisible ropes.

Supper was pleasant without being lavish. Father De Vroom was determined to take full advantage of so prolonged an interview with his superior, and Van Neercassel seemed genuinely interested in the life of a parish priest in Amsterdam, which afforded me the opportunity to just sit and listen. We retired early and rose early, and De Vroom joined Van Neercassel to celebrate early Mass. I would gladly have joined them if secrecy had not been an issue, so instead I passed the time in writing a further report for William in the hope that this would wrap matters up and I would be able to go back to my beloved books in Leiden. Given that William's army must be somewhere in the area, it might be possible to conclude the whole sorry affair in a day or two, and I began to sketch out my agenda for the next few days.

Monday morning — return to Amsterdam. Arrive mid-afternoon, God willing.
Proceed directly to retrieving the infants. Restore them to their parents.
Go to City Hall. Tell the mayors I have succeeded where they failed. Invite them to reconsider their position on William's taxes.
Receive their abject submission. Drop a note to William. And so to bed.

Tuesday morning — visit Jutte to thank her for her help and tell her of our successful conclusion. Maybe invite her to join me for a small dinner.

Tuesday afternoon — start out for Leiden. Travel into the night if necessary to get home quicker.

Tuesday night in my own bed.

Wednesday morning — have a lie-in so as not to think about Brother Anthony Francis being painfully dismantled on the scaffold. Maybe pray for his soul (if I am awake). Think about how I'm going to sweet talk the Bishop of Namur around my failure to wait upon him.

Twice in my life William had written me a letter that had proved very useful. The first had told anyone who read it that I was working for the Stadhouder and was to be given every assistance, otherwise they would answer to William. He had never asked me to return it and I kept it very safe because it was a useful thing to have. Admittedly the last time I had used it was with a cobbler who was being dilatory about repairing my boots, and it was not very effective then because he could not read, but it was a comfort to have it. The other letter was the one that he had written to the University of Leiden ordering them to give me a doctorate, which had got round the inconvenience of the then Rector threatening to demote me because I did not have one. I didn't use the title, because I felt a bit sheepish about the subterfuge, but I was grateful to him for that. I wondered idly whether there was anything that William could write to the Bishop of Namur that might help my cause. I couldn't think of it, and there might be some awkwardness in asking for a letter to a Catholic bishop in any event, especially a foreign one. One of the slurs regularly flung at Catholics in my country was that they were traitors because they owed allegiance to a foreign potentate, namely the Pope, so asking for a nice letter to one might just fuel the flames.

The two priests emerged to interrupt my train of thought. De Vroom looked refreshed and happy after Mass, while Van Neercassel drew me to one side.

'I thought it inappropriate to admit the friar to receive Communion until the infants have been found. He knows that if they are not retrieved he will die excommunicate, because I have told him so. Since I will not be with you, Father De Vroom has my authority to complete the excommunication on my behalf.'

This may seem like a small administrative nicety, but I assure you that to a devout Catholic the thought of dying excommunicate is terrifying. While you are excommunicated, you cannot receive the Blessed Sacraments. It is true that at the point of death these can be restored to you, but the friar could not know for certain that this would be possible. There might not be a priest around when one was needed.

'I hope, Master, that in the light of my wholehearted co-operation in this matter, the threat of further penal laws can be withdrawn?' Van Neercassel said.

'I am sure that I need make no such recommendation in my report to the Stadhouder,' I confirmed. I phrased it that way because it was not impossible that William would crack down on Catholics of his own volition once he heard that a friar had abducted the children, but at least I could honestly say that I had not recommended such a course of action. Anyway, Van Neercassel seemed satisfied with my response.

'Thank you, Master. I am sorry that this misguided young man has caused so much trouble. I need hardly say that the Catholic Church does not approve of forced conversions.'

I have no doubt that he was sincere, but you can be sincere and wrong. I am sure that he disapproved, but there were plenty of his colleagues who did not. Indeed, the Portuguese in Amsterdam were remnants of a people who had suffered forcible conversion. In the Americas native peoples were being coerced into Christianity; and, although we did not know it at the time, at that very moment the authorities in Goa were issuing laws making the use of Portuguese compulsory and requiring attendance at Christian churches.

I have to allow that I had known much of this before, but I had never really thought about it. Until I came to Amsterdam, I had never met people whose relatives had converted under duress. It did not shake my faith, but it rattled my allegiance. How could a God who epitomises love be the cause of such aggression? Surely only because his disciples — us — had misunderstood his message? Could I be a priest in a Church that would do this?

I had converted to Catholicism because I could not believe the doctrine of double predestination, the idea that some people were destined for Heaven or Hell from the moment of their coming into being. But now I felt that I could never represent the Catholic Church if it was doing this to infants. Since I was a secret priest I could just quietly stop doing anything, but I would have to explain myself to the Bishop; and if he felt vindictive he could denounce me to the authorities at Leiden. I would be dismissed, perhaps even degraded. What else could I do? I am a philosopher. Those skills are not much use for anything else, and there is no call for freelance philosophers.

Such thoughts crowded into my mind as we returned to Amsterdam. Hudde seemed equally pensive, while Father De Vroom was trying to read a book despite the wailing of the penitent friar in the cage behind us, not helped by the fact that Pringle was riding alongside him regaling him with accounts of public executions that he had witnessed.

To add to Anthony Francis's general air of dissatisfaction, it began to pour. The soldiers were kind enough to drape an oilcloth over the cage, though I doubt that it afforded him much protection. De Vroom and Hudde commenced a conversation as to whether excommunication automatically caused the expulsion of the Brother from the Franciscans and meant that he should revert to his original name. I could have told them that it did not, because excommunication is always meant to be temporary, the hope being that the sinner will confess his sins, make reparation or other penance and be restored to the fold, but since this would demonstrate an unhealthy and surprising grasp of Catholic doctrine I kept my mouth firmly shut.

I had shared the names and addresses of the couples who had received a Portuguese child with Hudde, who informed us that the addresses were not, as I feared, dispersed throughout Amsterdam, but were in the districts beyond the Prinsengracht. Fine houses, no doubt, and families who could afford to live there would not easily be cowed into giving the children up, for whom, I am sure, they would have paid handsomely, but Hudde breathed a sigh of relief to see that they were not among the leading families of the city, who could have made his job very difficult.

'In any case,' he opined, 'the law is on our side. They have received stolen property which must be restored to its owner, just as if they had been found with a clock or a painting. The fact that it has been bought and paid for makes no difference.'

'I have little sympathy for them,' I remarked, 'for they knew that they were entering into an irregular transaction.'

'I agree,' Hudde replied, 'but it is often those who know the fault lies with them who bleat loudest.'

'Should we go straight there?' I asked. 'A surprise would reduce the risk that they will hear somehow and hide the children.'

'They do not know that we are coming,' answered Hudde, 'and we hardly dare take the friar with us.'

That was a good point. I am certain that Anthony Francis was looking forward to being lodged in a nice dry dungeon somewhere. Glancing behind me I could see him kneeling in the cage, seemingly praying fervently as we went along.

De Vroom gave a gentle cough. He had been so quiet that I had almost forgotten that he was there. 'The saddest part of this horrible episode is that there are plenty of children in orphanages who would welcome a home. When we arrive, I will see what small children we have who could be offered in place of the Jewish infants,' he said.

The rain stopped, and so did we, to partake of a slim meal at a wayside inn. Anthony Francis declared that he had no appetite, and was unimpressed by Pringle's argument that he must eat so that he would have the strength to climb the scaffold on Wednesday morning, a suggestion that seemed to provoke the utmost distress in the young man.

The downpour earlier had made the road muddy, and on the last part of the journey we had to be pushed out of the mud twice. This slowed our progress and it was not until nearly six o'clock that we drew to a halt outside the City Hall.

By common consent it was not a good idea to reclaim the children in the dark. We would not know that we had the right child, I suppose, though my proposal that we should fetch the parents to make an identification was objected to by Pringle and Hudde, both of whom felt that it would introduce added emotions into a transaction that was sure to be fraught anyway. I could see their point of view, though I could not help but observe that it would be a great pity if we confiscated a child and delivered him to the Jewish quarter only to find that it was the wrong infant.

'But Master,' said Pringle, 'surely these people wanted children because they have none? We can be quite certain that any child of the right age that we find is likely to be one of those that we seek.'

Hudde summoned a couple of members of the civic guard to lock Brother Anthony Francis in a cell somewhere, charging them to ensure that there was no possibility of escape.

'Is he the one they're executing on Wednesday, Mayor?' asked one.

Hudde agreed that it was he.

'Caught him in the nick of time, then,' came the reply. 'I'd hate to think we'd spent all day building that bastard of a scaffold with nobody to put on it.'

Clearly diplomacy was not a prerequisite for membership of the civic guard, a point reinforced by his colleague, who was distinctly heard as they took the friar away to say that he had never seen a judicial disembowelling and was quite looking forward to it.

'I don't suppose you are,' he said to Brother Anthony Francis, not unkindly.

Father De Vroom said that he would walk to his church, because after such a journey he would relish the chance to stretch his legs, so we bade him a good night and only then did we enter the City Hall, tired after our long journey but content that we had done our duty.

We climbed the stairs to the main chamber and pushed the door open.

'Ah, there you are!' said the Stadhouder. 'I wondered when you'd turn up.'

CHAPTER TWENTY

My heart dropped to somewhere around my ankles. I had forgotten the Stadhouder's declared intention. He was not only the person I least expected to see here. He was also the one I least wanted to see just at that moment.

'Have you been here long, Your Excellency?' I asked as pleasantly as I could.

'A couple of hours,' said William. 'But I've been well entertained by these gentlemen.' He pointed at Geelvinck, Van Beuningen and Huydecoper. To judge by their expressions, you would think that they too were bound for the scaffold on Wednesday morning. 'I must thank you for your excellent dispatches,' William continued. 'I mean no reflection upon your abilities that it seemed convenient to come myself, since I was in the area.'

I introduced Hudde to him.

'We are old acquaintances, aren't we, mijnheer Hudde? So, tell us all how your mission went.'

I described the events in Utrecht as I have laid them out here. There is nothing to be gained by repeating them; besides which, I might contradict myself. It was a long time ago now. 'I propose to collect the children in the morning and restore them to their parents.'

William bounded to his feet. 'They've waited long enough, Mercurius! No time like the present.'

I cannot do with this sort of enthusiasm at the end of a long day, but I tried to feign keenness. 'As you direct, Stadhouder,' I said. 'Do you have your carriage here?'

'Of course not, but Pringle can find me a horse, can't you, Captain?'

'I'll bring two, Stadhouder. It would not do for the Master to ride in a carriage while you were on horseback.'

'Oh, I'm not worried about protocol and stuff like that,' William declared, in a pronouncement that was simultaneously extremely welcome and a complete lie.

'Perhaps mijnheer Pereyra should be here,' I suggested.

'Who? Oh, that Portuguese chap you mentioned. Yes, that would be good. And I'd like to meet him. He sounds like my sort of man.'

This was not a vulgar reference to any wicked proclivity, as some have alleged. I suspect that what William was getting at was that he might need a loan again one day and you can never have too many chests to raid.

'Well, don't stand there like a fifth hoof. Go and fetch the fellow. I'll amuse myself here until you get back.'

The mayors appeared less than overjoyed by that suggestion but forced a smile. Huydecoper suggested that some refreshments might be appropriate.

'Got any apples?' asked William.

The soldiers had just finished putting the carriage away when Pringle and I appeared to order them to get it ready again. This was greeted with all the delight that you might expect, but before long we were rolling out of the courtyard and heading towards the Jewish quarter.

I trust that I am not unreasonably prudish. Well, probably I am, actually. I have led a sheltered and orderly life. I am not a child; but as the carriage traversed Amsterdam by night I goggled at the depravity in this great city. Women disported themselves in brightly lit windows. I know what is alleged to have happened at Sodom, but until that evening I had no idea what might have gone on in Gomorrah. Not far from the City Hall there was the most flagrant display of vice imaginable. Not two hundred paces away! Right under the mayors' noses there were near naked women exhibiting themselves to anyone who passed by, and they appeared to have done nothing about it.

'Have you ever seen anything like this, Pringle?' I asked.

'As a matter of fact…' he began, and then proceeded to tell me of one of his adventures overseas in the most lurid detail. I was glad I had not eaten, especially when he mentioned the goat. [No, Van der Meer, I am not going to tell the tale. Some stories are better forgotten, if I ever can.]

I was heartily glad when we arrived at Pereyra's home and explained our purpose in coming. He snatched a coat and hat and we lost no time in retracing our steps. I was delighted to see that he was as discomfited by the exhibition in the waterside windows as I was. He put his hand over his eyes and began speaking Hebrew rapidly, which I took to be a sign of prayer.

Arriving at the City Hall, we found William waiting in front. I introduced Pereyra, who dropped to his knees and expressed the devotion of his people to the Stadhouder in effusive terms; not too many effusive terms, because William helped him up after a few moments.

'No time for that now, mijnheer. Now, gentlemen, Mijnheer Hudde will guide us, and I will collect the children personally for mijnheer Pereyra to identify. Onwards!'

He sprang on his horse — no small feat, because he was a small man and it was a large horse — and we clattered off over the cobbles, this time heading westwards. Fifteen minutes later, we arrived at the first house.

I will not describe the painful scenes that ensued at each successive house. As you might imagine, the arrival of an official party to remove one they thought of as their child was heart-breaking to the families, but it was good that the Stadhouder himself was there. Having twenty armed soldiers probably helped a bit too. The children were produced, identified by Pereyra, and placed in the carriage. This was where we had not thought matters through correctly, because at the subsequent stops I had to stay in the carriage with the babes while Hudde and Pereyra went inside, and as we returned to the Jewish quarter each of us had a small child on our laps; and since the children were themselves distressed and dumbfounded by this turn of events, soon we each had a wet child on our lap.

This did not seem to matter to the parents one bit. As the children were returned, they evidenced the deepest joy and bestowed blessings of every kind on the Stadhouder, which was a bit rich given that I had done all the work, but I believe that Pereyra subsequently explained the full story to them all.

It took some time to detach wailing women from the Stadhouder's arms, but eventually we were able to leave them to their rejoicing, something which apparently required everyone in the neighbourhood to be roused and to appear in the street with wine and honey cakes. I doubt their Christian neighbours got much sleep that night.

I found Pereyra dancing and explained that I proposed to return to Leiden at the earliest opportunity.

'What will happen to the Brother?' he asked.

'He is to pay for his sins with his life,' I explained. 'On Wednesday morning he will be executed on the Dam Square.'

'I wish it were not so,' said Pereyra.

'Do you deny that he deserves it?'

'No, of course not, Master. But tonight is one for rejoicing, and it will be overshadowed by the taking of life.'

I remembered that in the Easter story the chief priests had told Pilate that they had no law to put a man to death. This cannot have been strictly true, because it did not stop them stoning St Stephen later.

Pereyra broke away and ran over to where Hudde and William were talking. I did not follow, but after some animated discussion he returned, smiling.

'You seem happy,' I said.

'I am,' he replied. 'I have bought his life.'

I was flabbergasted. 'You've bought what?'

'I told our beloved Stadhouder that we wanted to show our appreciation by giving him a small present of a hundred guilders. In exchange, I begged that the friar would not die. He is to be sent to the East Indies as a missionary.'

Given the unhealthy climate in those parts it was still a death sentence of sorts, but at least he would keep his bowels inside his belly.

'But it is a municipal sentence. Have the mayors agreed?'

'Mijnheer Hudde says that he will convince them.'

No doubt Hudde would. I doubt that I could have done it.

'The friar is to be publicly branded on the arm in case he tries to return,' Pereyra continued, 'so the scaffold will not be completely wasted.'

I spotted William waving to me.

'Come along,' he said. 'We can't stand here gabbling all night. Affairs of state to attend to, you know.'

We waved goodbye to all and returned to the City Hall, where it was clear that the remaining mayors had been discussing something heatedly. We could hear raised voices as we climbed the stairs.

'Some bread and cheese would be welcome,' William announced as he flung the doors back.

'I'll organise it,' said Hudde, doubtless pleased not to be present for the next few minutes.

William sat in a chair and motioned us all to sit. Pringle remained standing by the door, his good eye firmly fixed on Huydecoper. I do not know if this unnerved the mayor, but if it had been directed at me little Shmuel Pimentel would not have been the only source of urine in my lap that evening.

We sat patiently waiting for Hudde to return. Servants bustled around us, giving us platters loaded with bread, butter and cheese. Once we had all been served, the servants withdrew and William smiled benignly.

'Now,' he said, 'tell me what you're doing about Panama.'

Geelvinck dropped his goblet. 'I didn't — we didn't...' he began.

'Hush!' commanded Van Beuningen.

'I hear that you have been listening to mijnheer Paterson's hare-brained scheme to carve a canal across the jungle there.'

'It has been discussed,' Van Beuningen conceded.

'And have you committed yourselves?'

'To a small degree,' Huydecoper interjected.

'I don't call twenty thousand guilders...' began Geelvinck before stopping to rub his ankle where Van Beuningen had just kicked it.

'You see,' said William suavely, 'quite apart from the technical imperfections of the plan, there is the difficulty that it lies in the territory of the Spanish king. And we have a treaty with Spain under which we are obliged to come to the aid of the other party in the event of an attack upon our lands. So you will grasp my dilemma; if a Dutchman were to garrison such a trading post, I am compelled by treaty to remove them by force. But if the post is not garrisoned, how long do you think it will survive?'

I report what William said. Of course, none of us knew the terms of any treaty with Spain, so he may have been making the whole thing up. You could never tell with the Stadhouder.

William was still smiling cheerily. Geelvinck was sweating profusely; Van Beuningen had developed a twitch in his cheek and had gone rather pale; Huydecoper's customary bullishness had evaporated; and Hudde, who seemed the least perturbed by this turn of events, was the first to speak.

'I think I speak for us all, Stadhouder, when I say that we were not aware of that, but of course it puts rather a different complexion on things. We can see now that this renders the scheme much less attractive.'

'That's good,' William beamed. 'I wouldn't want to upset Spain when we may need her help to tame our real enemy, France. No doubt we can now discuss the taxes that have been unaccountably delayed. Oh, before we do, I have something for you.' He waved his hand and Pringle handed him a package. 'We found this book, mijnheer Huydecoper. I believe it may belong to you.'

Now it was Huydecoper's turn to look pale.

'Let us not pretend that it was not fascinating. I'm sure some of those named would be interested to know how cheaply their friendship was valued and how much others of their acquaintance received. Of course,' William continued, 'in certain circumstances they need never know. That might be for the best. We wouldn't want any distractions to interfere with tax collecting, would we?'

'I suppose not,' growled Huydecoper.

'Excellent. Then here is your book.'

Huydecoper clutched it to his chest and then resumed his seat.

'If it goes missing again,' William smiled, 'it may be helpful to know that I have a copy.'

When we woke in the morning, we could see that William's men had finished trudging along the road at some point and were camped in Dam Square, which would have made the execution the following day somewhat problematic.

William was a soldier. He could sleep anywhere. In the event he put up at the same inn as Pringle, where he ordered me to join him for breakfast. I had packed my bags and loaded the carriage, and took my leave of mijnheer Hudde and his wife with grateful thanks for their hospitality.

I bowed as I approached William.

'You've done well, Master,' he said.

'I have? It seems to me I failed at several points.'

William shook his head. 'You got the taxes, with a bit of help. You found out what the English were up to. And you solved an abduction and returned the children to their loving families. Not only that, I got a hundred guilders towards my considerable expenses. And I now have quite a hold over the mayors here. Two holds, in fact. Huydecoper's book and the adventure in Panama are both things they do not choose to have bruited abroad. I am well content. In fact, I think you should have the hundred guilders.'

'Your Excellency, that was paid to purchase a man's life. I do not think I can take blood money.'

'That's very moral of you, Mercurius. Very few of my servants decline money. I wish there were more of you. Is there anything else I can do for you?'

Inspiration struck. I firmly believe that I could again feel the hand of Providence upon my shoulder. 'Yes, Stadhouder. You wouldn't like to ban me from leaving the country without your permission? For, shall we say, three years?'

The Stadhouder's letter was perfect for my needs, as it should have been, because I wrote it. He was good enough to suggest a phrase that described me as 'an adviser so important' that I could not be spared to proceed abroad where 'ill-disposed elements' might kidnap or kill me to deprive the Stadhouder of my wise counsel. He was kind enough to sign two copies so that I could send one to the Bishop of Namur with my regrets that I could not attend upon him without the consent of the Stadhouder who, being a staunch Calvinist, was unlikely to give it so that I could visit a Catholic bishop.

I had to abandon my fanciful idea of having dinner with Jutte, since I could not expect the military escort to wait outside, but I knocked at the Begijnhof and sat awhile with her in the peace of the garden.

'The children are all returned safely, so my task here is complete,' I explained.

She nodded serenely. 'I am glad to hear it,' she said. 'It weighed upon my conscience that I had in any measure abetted a kidnapper of children.'

'You were not to know,' I said. 'Some religious people are not trustworthy, I'm afraid.'

She sat for at least a count of five before replying. 'I think you may be trustworthy, Master.'

'You hardly know me.'

'True, but a woman has to develop that sense. The weaker sex cannot afford to get these things wrong too often.'

'Were you married?' I asked.

'Yes, for twelve years. He died two years ago of a fever. I came here to find peace.'

'Did you have children?'

'Two. My mother cares for them. One day I may return to the outside world and resume my life there, but not just yet, I think.'

'How will you survive?'

'I have learned some crafts here. And my husband left me well provided for. My mother has the use of my money for now.'

Now it was my turn to count to five. 'Will you marry again?'

'I don't think so. I already have children and this house offers me security. Why would I marry?'

Why indeed? I thought, and went on thinking it all the way home.

A NOTE TO THE READER

Dear Reader,

I hope you have enjoyed reading this book as much as I enjoyed researching and writing it. If you have, please tell your friends. Get yourself some new friends so you can tell them too.

It was all kicking off in 1684. Amsterdam really did withhold its taxes, and following the Rye House plot's failure a number of English refugees came to live there. William Paterson later launched his Panama (or Darién) scheme in Scotland and came close to bankrupting the country. William III is often criticised for obstructing it, but it isn't widely known that he had heard of it before.

This book had its genesis when I read about Huydecoper's book, which is exactly as I describe it. He recorded all the gifts he gave or received, and it occurred to me that this could have been embarrassing for him if it fell into the wrong hands. Add to that the mass of information in Steven Nadler's book about the Jews of Amsterdam, and I had plenty to weave into a story.

People occasionally ask about the background for my stories. The books I used include:

The Dutch Golden Age, by Hans Goedkoop and Kees Zandvliet

The Dutch Moment, by Wim Klooster

Rembrandt's Jews, by Steven Nadler

Dutch Ships in Tropical Waters, by Robert Parthesius

The Dutch Republic in the Seventeenth Century, by Maarten Prak

The Wisdom of the Beguines, by Laura Swan

Strategic Affection? Gift Exchange in Seventeenth-Century Holland, by Irma Thorn

The Price of Scotland: Darien, Union and the Wealth of Nations, by Douglas Watt

There is a fascinating animation of the expansion of Amsterdam in the 17th century at: **https://www.iamexpat.nl/expat-info/dutch-expat-news/video-expansion-amsterdam-17th-century**.

If you have enjoyed this novel, I'd be really grateful if you would leave a review on **Amazon** and **Goodreads**. I love to hear from readers, so please keep in touch through **Facebook** or **Twitter**, or leave a message on my **website**.

Dank je wel!

Graham Brack

Sapere Books is an exciting new publisher of brilliant fiction and popular history.

To find out more about our latest releases and our monthly bargain books visit our website:
saperebooks.com

38730748R00124